Drivers

Peter Carroll

Raven Crest Books

ISBN-13: 978-0-9929387-0-3

ISBN-10: 0-99-293870-8

For Sharon and Megan

1.

Too right I'm bricking it. You would be too, if you were in my shoes. He's not a man to be messed with. Too late for that, mind you. Too late for regrets or second thoughts; I acted on the first thought and, as far as he's concerned, that forfeits my right to a follow-up. There will be no redemption through apology either. All I can look forward to is an enormous helping of pain - if he ever catches up with me.

So it's simple, right: don't get caught.

Aye.

Simple.

No, of course it's not simple but, then again, tell me something in life that is?

Oh, aye, me. I'm simple. Must be. Stands to reason; I'm short of brain cells. That's the cause of my current predicament. Oh, and her.

Aye, she's to blame as well. If she hadn't been so gorgeous, so persuasive, so unhinged, I might not be here.

Might not. Always hard to say with such things. I'm a *bona fide* screw-up in my own right. I've got form. Blaming her suits me. Deflects from the defects. Detracts from the artefacts.

I realise you have no idea who he is or who she is but - patience my friend - there are more pressing matters for me to attend to.

The smoke is still twisting upwards. Languid. Serpentine. The smell reminds me of the caps I fired from a toy gun as a kid. A roll of red paper, punctuated with evenly spaced dots of gunpowder; the same acrid, sweet smell as now, when each tiny charge exploded with a snap under the hammer of the gun; each blackened remnant creeping out of the top of the barrel. When you had no gun, you'd hit them with a stone just for the joy of hearing them crack. Some guys would try and set off a big bunch all at once, hoping to create a small fire in the process. Only, this isn't kids' stuff. This is all too real. There's no disputing whether or not I've shot this guy. There's not going to be any stomping off in the huff because he refused to die as directed and, even if he did lay down and expire, no Lazarus impersonation when his mammy calls him home for his tea.

No. This guy's tea's oot as they say in Glasgow. He's brown bread - if your preference is for Cockney rhyming slang. Or, he's fucked, if you're being completely blunt in any of our wonderfully diverse English-speaking enclaves.

I just shot Ralph Bonner in the face and it's not a pretty sight. Actually, he wasn't a pretty sight before – a kind of bulldog/human cross. It's fair to say I've not improved his looks any, though. I've never seen a dead person so close up before. I've never actually seen a dead person before in real life, as opposed to on the television or in the cinema. It's bizarre. Hard to take seriously. I'm looking into this guy's head. Not in the metaphorical sense of how a shrink might look into it, but literally, right inside it. The bullet has wreaked havoc. Blood is spreading out behind him, creating a glistening slick halo. I think I should be moving, getting the hell out of there but I can't. I'm staring, entranced, frozen to the spot. I can't really take in the enormity of what's just happened. This is a big moment: a Rubicon crossed, another of normality's bridges going up in flames.

I snap out of my trance. There's noise, a commotion somewhere. Far enough off to give me some time, I hope.

I'm feeling scared again. The adrenalin that fuelled the despatching of Ralph is receding. This plan, if that's what you can really call it, doesn't seem such a good idea any more. I can feel the tingling heat of The Stickman's ire. I'm bricking it. But, as I said, you would be too. I guarantee it.

I have to go but I can't leave this bloody mess behind. I have enough to worry about without adding the police into the mix.

I turn Ralph over. No exit wound. The diffusing blood all seems to be coming from the gaping hole in the front of his head. The bullet is lodged inside somewhere. Thick skull – I'm saying nothing.

I'm mindful of evidence trails; ballistics matching bullets and guns to each other. I shove the gun into my waistband and I delve. It's not pleasant. He's still warm; crunches, squelches. Retching, trying not to look, I finally locate the hard lump of shrapnel I planted there a few moments ago and pull it out. I wrap the bullet in a bit of paper tissue, put it in my pocket. I'll find a place to dispose of it later.

I have a sudden bout of guilt in regard to Ralph's mother; I'm making her job of identifying the body literal because, thanks to me, the face only she could love has been replaced with a lump of gelatinous bloody gloop. But it's not my fault Mrs B - he was trying to kill me. I was just defending myself; he gave me no choice.

I look around. There's a motorbike parked between a couple of cars. I drag Ralph over toward it by the ankles. He weighs a frigging ton, thick round the middle as well as between the ears. A bloody snail-trail smears across the ground behind him.

I tip the bike on its side and use the rather impressive knife he pulled on me to dislodge the fuel cap. Petrol spills out across Ralph's upper body and legs. I stand the bike back up again, feeling bad about damaging it as it's a great looking machine. I would so love to just ride off into the sunset on it. Two issues there: no keys, and no clue how to ride a bike, even if someone handed them to me right then.

The knife goes back into the holster inside his jacket. The gloves come off, pulled inside out, stuffed into one of Ralph's pockets. I take out my lighter. Click, whoosh, he's

3

up, up and away.

The smell is awful: cheap clothing melting, encouraging the flames. I'm looking about again. Sooner or later, someone will come back for the bike or one of the cars. I can't wait around. I need to go. I should have been better prepared to deal with eventualities; haven't done a very good job of keeping the scene of Ralph's facial obliteration clean. I've no real faith in this fire as a foolproof deterrent to detection but it seemed worth a try.

Thing is, a fire wasn't exactly the best way to remain undetected - it's a bit of an attention grabber. It would seem that I don't react well under pressure. Improvisation's not turning out to be my strong suit.

I've been stepping back. Instinct and subconscious self-preservation must have been pulling on an invisible rope to draw me away, pull me clear.

I'm about ten metres from the burning body of a man I just shot in the face.

Now, I run.

2.

The alleyway is a dead-end. That might turn out to be rather too apt.

His head goes left, centre, right, centre, left, centre, up. Repeat.

Sheer brick cliffs close in and stretch skywards on three sides. On the wall straight ahead is a solid, handle-less, black door with a green and white sign identifying it as a 'Fire Exit'. It's also of the opinion that he should 'Keep Clear'. The door gives up nothing to his shoulder. In contrast, his shoulder almost gives up to the door. Should have taken more notice of the notice. A few unlit windows taunt him – the majority of which are barred. Even the ones that don't belong in a prison, set lowest down, look like they'll be just too high to reach. A running, scrambling jump confirms his suspicions. In any case, there's no chance any of these windows will be open; no chance of one being left ajar in case someone needed to make good their escape.

He scans the ground for a weapon. A wooden pallet and a grey plastic chair with black metal legs are the best his rat-trap has to offer. There's not even a decent-sized rock or a discarded bottle. The chair is a flimsy, lightweight affair. The pallet looks spit-through brittle. Neither option will induce trepidation in those chasing him. He breaks off a chunk of pallet, swishes it through the air like a sword. Might as well.

As the rain falls through frigid winter air, his breath clouds with every heavy exhalation of attempted recovery.

Adrenalin drove him down here, into this cul de sac, much faster than them. Part man, part whippet; baby he was born to run. Running from The Boss. Oh, the irony.

The most frustrating thing is that if he'd made a better choice of right turns he'd be away, gone, *adiós amigos*. Only these particular *amigos* ain't his *amigos* any more. He shat in his own nest and they are intent on handing down a harsh lesson in the importance of maintaining higher standards of domestic hygiene. It was a stupid and vain thing, to skim off some merchandise for his own fledgling operation. But it was done. No point crying over spilt milk - even if it was more likely to be spilt blood. His blood.

Clattering heavy footsteps; multiple runners slowing to walk.

They are here.

Swish, swish.

Pish.

"Tommy? You down here, you thieving shitebag?"

Mick Shearer. Enforcer, hard man, head case. Amigo no more.

The alleyway is not well lit, but well enough lit to reveal their quarry.

"Oh dear, Tommy. You seem to have taken a wrong turn back there, son. What a shame. So close to getting away, too. So close."

He can see three others with Shearer. Jimmy McLean, Rab Sweeney and Wee Baz. He didn't know Baz's surname. Never bothered to ask – it didn't seem all that important before. Certainly not important right at this moment. What he does know is that all four are trouble in their own right. In combination, he can expect the worst. His endocrine system provided him with fleetness of foot in flight, now it was time for it to stoke the fire in his muscles to fight.

The four former colleagues advance, shoulder to shoulder, like gunslingers headed for a shoot-out but without the guns ... maybe. One of them could well be packing. Mick had a reputation for carrying - well-earned, as it happened. On more than one occasion, Tommy looked on, detached, uninterested in the condemned man's

6

fate as Shearer administered a sentence passed down by The Boss. A different kind of detachment was likely to be on the cards tonight.

Tommy's as far back into the alley as he can go, the broken fragment of pallet looking about as intimidating as a toothpick. At least a toothpick served a useful purpose. Maybe he could give one of them a splinter? Might get infected and they'd die of blood poisoning. The Scots call splinters *'skelfs'*. Thanks to his slim build he often found himself described thus as a child. Maybe if he bit them he'd cause the blood poisoning? He laughs at the absurdity of his twisted thought processes. Stress is a wonderful thing as far as the imagination is concerned.

Sweeney lets something drop into his hand from inside his sleeve. A cut-down baseball bat. Oh, good.

"Seriously, Tommy, what the fuck is that you're holding? Hang on boys, stand back, he's got a bit of pallet and he's not afraid to use it!" says McLean, spreading his arms across the front of two of his three companions, pretending to halt their progress.

Three of them laugh. Shearer doesn't crack a light: the epitome of focus; a humourless prick.

Tommy doesn't wait for them to get any closer. He takes a chance; runs forward, hurls the chair at Wee Baz with no surname, tries to squirm past him as he ducks to avoid the makeshift missile. It nearly works. He's past Wee Baz with no surname and ready to sprint, to outrun these lumbering gorillas with ease, again. So near, but the epitome of focus was ready for him. The punch from the humourless prick sends him spinning sideways, vision blurring, legs buckling. Sweeney's bat finishes the job. He's sprawling, face skidding along the ground, nose crumpling - the first proper dose of pain.

McLean hauls him up off the ground and the blows rain down like pistons. The first few hurt like fuck, but after the sixth or tenth or fifteenth, he's so dazed and numb, they make no difference. Tommy can tell bits of him are getting damaged; blood oozing from more than one wound, but it's like an out-of-body experience. He's looking down on someone else getting a doing here. Except they're not and he most definitely is. For the first time, he blacks out.

He wakes to find he's sitting in the chair he threw at Wee Baz with no surname. Wee Baz is, of course, well over six foot: nicknames in Scotland tending toward the ironic whenever possible. The four henchmen of his apocalypse are arranged in a semi-circle in front of him. Front and centre is Mick Shearer.

"Well, I've got to give you some credit for having a go, Tommy. Showed a bit of bottle there, son. You can run as well. Like a bloody gazelle, so you were. Thing is, we'd have got to you eventually. You were only delaying the inevitable. You can't take gear off The Boss and expect to get away with it. I mean, you know that well enough. You've seen what happens to guys who cross him."

Tommy coughs. A bubble of blood bursts between his swollen lips; pain surges through his battered body but he refuses to show it. These guys thrive on exploiting weakness, enjoy the suffering of others – one of the perks of their job. He wouldn't be pleading or begging. If he made it through this, they'd regret it. It might take a while but he'd get each of them alone and repay them a thousand times over.

Idle threats.

Aye, maybe.

For now.

We'll see.

"You got nothing to say for yourself, Tommy?" asks Sweeney.

Tommy looks at him with his right eye, his left has closed, shakes his head as much as the pain will allow.

Shearer is pacing back and forth a few steps at a time, not covering any significant distance.

Stops.

Walks forward.

"I spoke to The Boss this morning, Tommy, asked him what he wanted me to do with you. What do you think he said?"

Tommy tries to shrug but it doesn't come to much, feels like his left shoulder might be dislocated. Coughs again. Another burst bubble. He winces, groans. Can't keep it down.

"*Give him a hiding,* he says. *A proper going over. Hospital but not the cemetery.* Really? Is that it? I says to him. Just a good old-fashioned shoeing? *Aye,* says he. *Something permanent, though. Not just a broken jaw,*" Shearer grabs Tommy by the face and squeezes another groan out of him, "*something to remember me by, a parting gift so to speak.*"

The other three are smiling, chuckling, relishing. Shearer reaches into his jacket and pulls out the gun. Tommy recoils instinctively and the chair topples, taking him backwards along with it. He hits the floor with a lot more force than his dilapidated body can cope with. The air rushes from him, his battered ribcage struggling to regain control of his lungs. Three of them laugh and one of them remains as stone but Tommy won't panic, won't let them see his fear. He's been here before. His father couldn't take his dignity; sure as fuck these worthless errand boys weren't getting it.

He blacks out again.

When he wakes, McLean, Wee Baz with no surname and Sweeney have gone. He's upright in the chair, looking through the slit of his right eye at the barrel of the gun. That's all he can focus on. A black hole, drawing all of his attention with its immense gravitational pull. He doesn't register Shearer's presence. It's just Tommy and the gun. Tommy Gun.

A bang and a flash of light.

Pain like nothing so far; he's on his back again and his knee has gone.

"See you around, Tommy."

'You will,' thinks Tommy.
You will.

3.

I first met Tommy 'Stickman' Stevens at my old man's funeral. I was five.

You won't be too surprised to hear that it ranks as one of the worst days of my life. I can still conjure up the confusion, the bewilderment. Those feelings, emotions - much stronger than any visual recall. Platitudes and stupid lies about my daddy waiting for me in heaven or being up in the sky with Jesus spilled from the mouths of adults with no idea how to explain death to a child in rational straightforward terms.

I never knew my dad very well; a transient figure in my life. At least, I assume he was, given the paucity of fond memories I can draw upon when thinking about him. Occasional flashes of memory return to me but they form shadows, blurred lines; an incomplete jigsaw. My mum wasn't much use in that department either. Still isn't. She doesn't talk about him; said they were ill-suited and if he hadn't died, she'd have left him. Her motto seems to be: *if you've nothing good to say, say nothing.* To lose your old man when you're so young is hard because you don't know how to hold onto memories, or even that you should try to because they'll seem more important to you later in life. I've got a couple of old photos but they don't spark any marked improvement in my recall.

It is what it is, the hand dealt to me. I've learnt to live with it.

The day itself was cold. I'd been forced into an ill-fitting suit, borrowed from a cousin, with a tie that gripped my neck like the unwelcome hand of a stranger. Nothing seemed normal or right about it but, at that age, you haven't the knowledge or experience to make sense of it.

You do as you're told; you trail along, you don't understand why.

There were a lot of people there. I remember the feeling of being surrounded by giants. A forest of sombre trees. To be fair, most folk don't take small kids to funerals, for all the reasons given - unless it's one of their parents that have bitten the dust. And one of mine had.

I'd been presented to dozens of these well-meaning but emotionally incompetent mourners. The men in particular, out of their depth in terms of expressing their own feelings, never mind empathising with a five year old child. The women trying too hard to console me. Some of them were well known to me, a few I recognised but couldn't have named, and the rest were total strangers. I remember the palpable tension in my mother's voice and mannerisms as she introduced me to *him*. It was different to any of the others and that's why it stuck with me.

"Ross, this is Mr Stevens. Say hello."

I cowered into her side as he towered over me. The nickname was dual-purpose: he walked with a stick on account of some kind of leg injury; and he was six-foot-four and rail thin. The crooked smile revealed poorly maintained teeth, like a row of old tombstones. Appropriate. It was a smile with a sinister quality, conveying menace rather than amusement or pleasure. His eyes seemed to drill right through me in hard metallic grey – a kind of cold I'd never experienced before or since. At least, not from a human being.

The walking stick looked like an extension of his arm; a clear distinction only provided by an ornate snake's-head handle. An entirely befitting decoration; he looked part snake himself with that lithe frame and those dead eyes. I'd learn later he was every bit as poisonous, and deadly to boot.

"Alright, son," he growled. "I was sorry to hear about your daddy."

His voice transmitted the same glacial menace as his

smile. I fully expected his tongue to start flicking out between his neglected dentition, tasting the air, searching for unwary prey. Now I can imagine how a gerbil feels when a rattler comes calling. He definitely unsettled my mother, who trembled as he spoke.

"Anyway, that's me away, Anne. I'll see you later."

She didn't reply, merely nodding and pulling me in closer to her body.

The Stickman moved off, his derelict knee-joint rendering his gait awkward. His gangling frame added to the inelegance. By all accounts, you would be well-advised not to fall into the trap of thinking this made him easy to run from. I should have heeded that advice.

"Who was that man, Mammy? He was scary."

"Shush, Ross, don't be rude. He might hear you," she replied. "He's just a man who knew your daddy and came to pay his respects."

As first meetings go it was short, but no less memorable for its brevity.

***

I was eighteen and clubbing in earnest since I got my ID and could avoid the ignominy of being refused entry or service at the bar. This place was not one of my usual haunts but proved a good choice: banging music, friendly atmosphere, rammed to the rafters. Whatever its capacity as far as the authorities were concerned, the current management were exceeding it by a handsome margin. Christ knows what would have happened if a fire broke out. Thing is, when you're young and full of drink, such considerations are far from your mind. When you're young, male, full of drink and surrounded by a plethora of scantily-clad young women, forced into the close proximity of your person by the owner's disregard for such weighty matters as 'Health and Safety', you're even less likely to quibble.

She was dancing with three friends - or, at least, she was doing her best approximation of a dance in the space they squeezed into. I wasn't too bothered whether or not this was a fair representation of her abilities in relation to dancing. No, as far as I was concerned, she could have been dad-dancing at a wedding and it would have made no difference to my levels of arousal. As I said: the place was rammed; there were lots of beautiful women in there - but she was the only person I was taking any notice of.

"Hey, Ross. You want a drink, mate?"

I didn't hear my pal Gerry 'Big Mac' McDonald ask the question. Even the driving, thunderous dance music was being drowned out by my pounding heart. Enthralled and terrified in equal measure, I stared at the vision in front of me.

"Rosco? You want a drink, mate?" he bellowed again, most likely thinking it was merely the music preventing me from responding.

Still I failed to register his offer, so he grabbed me by the shoulder and used sign-language. I snapped out of my trance.

"Aye, cheers. I'll take a vodka and coke."

"What?"

"Vodka and coke, cheers."

"Right, no bother."

As Big Mac struggled off through the throng, heading to the bar, I stood there, watching her. Swirling and twisting, hair tumbling from her head like a golden waterfall. And then it happened: she looked over and caught me gawping. It wouldn't surprise me if I was open-mouthed. Just the hint of a smile, more of a smirk maybe, then a confab with her pals resulting in much amusement.

Bastard!

Caught, and having the proverbial ripped out of me.

Gutted, I headed for the toilet.

The lavatorial facilities in the club were poor, with piss and hand-towels vying for which could gain the greatest share of floor space. Cracked mirrors, dirty urinals and stalls more suited to a farmyard than a club. All this squalor ensured visits were limited to emergencies only. This counted. Not an emergency of the bowel or bladder variety, more an emergency of the heart and ego variety. I managed an unenthusiastic piss but couldn't take my mind off her. I'd need to go back out. Even if I could have withstood the smell, hanging about the bogs in a Glasgow club is likely to bring a whole set of other problems with it. In any case, I had a drink on its way, courtesy of my big mate Gerry. I needed to get a grip and get back out there.

She was walking away from Gerry, squeezing between lucky bastards, back towards her mates. I felt sick.

"Alright, Gerry," I said taking the proffered alcohol. "Who was that?"

"You mean you don't know?"

"No, I've no idea. I know she's a fucking stunner, mind you!"

I necked the drink, hoping it might steady my nerves; slow my pulse rate.

"Holy shit, Ross, that's Victoria Stevens."

I shook my head and shrugged, none the wiser.

"She's The Stickman's lassie."

My pounding heart almost burst right then. More than a dozen years had passed since my encounter with Tommy Stevens at my dad's funeral, but it wasn't just the memory of that first meeting, jolting through my synapses like a jump start, which filled me with apprehension. In the intervening period, I, like most other people in Glasgow, got to know all about The Stickman and his exploits via pub-based apocryphal tales and acres of lurid tabloid coverage of his alleged nefarious activities.

"Really? How do you know her, then?"

Big Mac was a bit of a dark horse. I'd known the boy for just over a year but, almost every time we ventured out on the town, I learnt something new or unexpected about him. He smiled. A smile to convey many things other than the full truth of the matter.

"She's pally with my sister, Sian. You've not met her yet, have you?"

I shook my head.

"Aye, well, they went to the same dancing classes. I used to try and chat Vicki up when me and my ma went to collect Sian. Well, until I found out who she was and then I backed right off."

He grinned. A more open gesture, lacking the subterfuge of his smile.

"Which is what you should do!" he said.

"What do you mean?"

"Oh, come off it, man. You're going to need a towel to wipe up all that drool and you were practically pitching a tent in your drawers watching her dance earlier!"

Gerry guffawed, slapped me on the back.

"Fuck off!" was the best I could manage in my defence. Mainly because he was right and I didn't have any defence.

I looked back over to where she'd been dancing.

She was gone.

My heart stopped.

4.

The pain of rehab channelled Tommy's mind toward the task in hand, toward resolution and reparation. Sure, he'd been wrong to take The Boss's gear and try to make a few quid on the side - even if, in reality, it was more like a down payment on his own entrepreneurial venture than a theft. You might call it a business loan...of sorts. In hindsight, asking may have been a better course of action than procuring without permission. Might have prevented his left knee from becoming an unexpected and unwelcome part of the settlement. If the knee was the capital, then the interest consisted of two cracked ribs, together with a broken nose, right hand, jaw, and collar bone. However, despite all that pain and misery, The Boss made a big mistake: Tommy still drew breath without the help of a machine.

The Boss probably thought he'd dealt with Tommy; that he'd never see him again. In the case of most people, getting the shit so comprehensively kicked out of you, combined with having your knee destroyed by a bullet, would be more than enough discouragement. A clear and unequivocal demonstration of who one should, and should not, fuck with.

Most people, yes.

Tommy ...

Weeks of flexing, stretching, lifting weights and manipulation were followed by endless hours in the swimming pool until, eventually, he moved onto walking. Despite heroic efforts on the part of all concerned, no amount of physical therapy could change the fact that he'd need a stick. The joint was shattered, ligaments torn asunder, and he wasn't a highly paid football player availed of unlimited funds. No matter, he'd turn that to his advantage somehow – he was a very resourceful young man.

Hours were spent pondering, plotting, and he decided on a very specific course of action. They would be dealt with one by one. The starting point would be Mick Shearer.

Mick Shearer liked a bet. In fact, it would be fair to describe him as a problem gambler. The main problem was his reaction to losing. He was about as bad a loser as it was possible to be. Although he wasn't really a very good winner either – not that he got to prove it all that often. The list of activities he wouldn't have a little flutter on was short; whilst dog and horse races ranked high among his favourite things on which to place wagers. When not carrying out his master's bidding in terms of violent requital, he could be found throwing away his ill-gotten gains in the bookies near his flat; a copy of the Racing Post in his hands, a tiny pencil behind his ear. The strange thing was, no matter how much angst and stress it appeared to cause him as far as onlookers were concerned, he found gambling therapeutic.

Tommy sat watching from the passenger seat of the Transit. His brother, Paul, occupied the driver's seat, fingers clenching and unclenching on the steering wheel, the leather creaking as it stretched. New gloves concealing warm, sweaty hands.

"You sure he's in there, Tommy?"

"Oh, aye, he's in there, Paul. Just relax, we could be here for quite a while. There's no hurry."

Paul exhaled loudly.

"I really need to have a smoke, Tommy."

"Look, I've told you, I don't want you smoking in the van. It stinks the place out."

"But, I'm gasping here, man."

"Oh, for fuck's sake. Alright, get out and have a bloody

fag then. Jesus wept!"

Paul didn't need any further encouragement: the cigarette was lit and the first draw taken before both feet were on the pavement and the door closed. The tension of his craving subsided in a soothing wave.

Darkness crept up on them as they sat waiting for Shearer to show. Light rain twisted through the orange beams of the street lights, each passing car's tyres produced a gentle swish as they cut through the gathering surface water. Paul pulled the collar of his coat up and ducked into the doorway of a tenement, the overhang of the lintel providing a modicum of shelter. He'd agreed to help his big brother without any hesitation. There were two years between them. Paul stood a bit shorter than Tommy – as did most folks – but was much heftier in build, establishing himself as someone not to be messed with. He knew Mick Shearer, knew his reputation, saw what he'd done to Tommy. It didn't faze him. A few different men shared his mother's house as he grew up. One of them may well have been his father, although there were no guarantees given his Mother's appetite for alcohol and casual sex. All of them had seen fit to use him and Tommy as punch bags, or worse. Apart from the last one, who'd tried to but came out second best. Throughout all the bad times, they'd stuck together: Paul and Tommy, brothers in harms.

"Bastard nag!"

Mick Shearer tore up his betting slip and threw the shredded paper upwards, letting it flutter to the floor like confetti. He knew this irked the shop owner, wee Paddy McCorkle, but he also knew the chicken-shit little tattie-howker didn't have the balls to say anything, never mind do anything, about it. Small demonstrations of power such as this helped Shearer feel better when things didn't go as planned. Although, he did wish he could avoid the frequent need for it in this place. He stood, slipped his coat on, and went for the door.

"See you tomorrow, Paddy."

"I bloody hope not," muttered McCorkle. Shearer should have been every bookie's delight: a mug punter *par excellence*, helping to boost Paddy's profits every time he crossed the threshold. But he negated any monetary advantage that might bring by behaving like a menacing bear with a temper on a hair trigger. Paddy genuinely feared for his life on more than one occasion when the incompetent bastard lost yet another bet and, as a result, a pile of cash. He sometimes wondered what he'd done in a past life to deserve such an affliction.

"Eh?"

"Aye, sure enough, Mick. I said I'll see you tomorrow, so I will. You go easy, now."

Shearer stepped out into the street and lit a cigarette. He stood for a moment, looking around. It paid to be aware of your surroundings in his game; to be ready for any eventuality. The rain hastened his mental processing; hurrying him on his way.

Tommy signalled to Paul, who crushed the remains of his second cigarette under his toe and got back into the van.

"We'll just sit here for a minute. He only lives a few hundred yards away. If he's going home we'll soon be able to tell," said Tommy.

"Fair enough."

Shearer used his Racing Post as a makeshift umbrella but, given the swirling wind, it didn't provide much respite from the now-torrential downpour. He broke into a semi-jog before abruptly ducking through a doorway and disappearing from view.

"Flat it is, then," said Paul.

"Looks like it. You ready for this, bro'?"

"Too right I am, Tommy. That prick Shearer's got it coming. Let's get up there and get this done."

Tommy pulled on his gloves, patted his pockets. He had the necessary. Zipping up his jacket, he pulled on a woolly hat in preparation for braving the elements. He grabbed the door handle, checking the wing mirror for any traffic before opening the door onto the road.

"Right then, let's go."

The doorbell rang just as Shearer switched on his kettle. He wasn't expecting visitors but sometimes his sister would drop in for a chat without giving prior notice, so it could be her. All the same, he tensed in readiness; his enemies were legion.

Shearer looked through the spyhole.

Nothing.

He opened the door a fraction and could see a small fire licking upwards from a bundle of newspaper on the floor of his close. He opened the door wider and looked about. Nothing. Kids – hoping he'd rush out, stamp on the paper to extinguish the flames, only to find they'd wrapped dog shit in it. The upshot being: they soil their pants from the hilarity of watching him soil his footwear.

"Aye, very good, you shower of bawbags. You'll need to do better than that to catch me out," he shouted down the close.

Shearer headed back to the kitchen for a glass of water to douse the shitty conflagration.

The brothers slipped from their hiding place in the stairwell. Paul stamped on the paper, then he and Tommy slipped into the flat, closed the door behind them.

Shearer took a pint glass from a cupboard, running the cold tap for a few seconds before filling it. He never heard them approach thanks to the combined noise of the running water and the now-boiling kettle. He did feel the whack of Tommy's stick against his skull, tried to unscramble his thoughts too late, and dropped like a sack of spuds when the second blow connected with his temple.

"Ok, let's truss this bastard up," said Tommy.

They tied Shearer's ankles and wrists, gagged him and pulled a bag over his head. Tommy went back down into the street to the van and drove it around to the back of the tenement block where Shearer lived.

Tommy returned to the flat to help Paul carry Shearer. He took the feet; Paul grabbed him under the armpits. They hefted him down the stairs, out into the rear alleyway and dumped him into the back of the Transit. They'd waited for dark and put on balaclavas but they didn't have to worry too much about being observed: this was the kind of neighbourhood where people turned a blind eye to such goings-on. It was not in the interests of the residents' long-term health to notice such things, never mind report them to the authorities.

Shearer's head throbbed as he regained consciousness. A dull, thudding ache, kept company by a localised stinging from the area of impact. He rolled his head around on his shoulders, trying to loosen his leaden muscles; get blood flowing back to his brain; clarify his thoughts. Hands and ankles were bound; head covered; sitting rather than lying down. Soaked through, he began to shiver in realisation at how cold he felt.

The bag came off without warning, revealing Tommy and Paul Stevens to be his captors.

"Fuck me, it's the Brothers Grimm, and by grim, I mean fucking dead!" snarled Shearer.

Paul delivered a smashing right-hander that sent Shearer flying sideways off his seat. He landed awkwardly, thanks to his bonds, face planted into the floor and right arm almost wrenched out of its socket by the impact. As the stars cleared, Shearer looked about him, spitting out a glob of blood and sputum. Wherever he was, the place looked unfamiliar. And yet....

"Shut the fuck up, Shearer, you piece of shit," said Paul, shaking his hand and stretching his fingers to relieve the pain he'd just inflicted upon himself: the punch a little over-enthusiastic - the next day's x-ray would reveal a broken bone.

The brothers pulled Shearer back up into a sitting position.

"You better enjoy your cheap shots while you can, Paulo, coz when I get these ropes off I'm going to knock every one of your teeth down your throat before I slit it, you cowardly fuck."

"You think I'm scared of you, Shearer? Eh? Tommy, untie this ugly fucker and let me loose on him."

Tommy stood, leaning on his stick with one hand, the other pushed deep into his coat pocket. The rain hammered down but he remained oblivious to the drenching it delivered.

"Paul, mate, don't rise to it. This is between me and him."

"Ha, Tommy Stevens. What is it they call you now? '*Stickman*'? It suits you, you lanky prick. I thought you'd learned your lesson, son. I thought taking your knee would have told you all you needed to know about what happens to folk who fuck with The Boss or The Boss's team."

"Aye, it taught me plenty, Mick. The main thing being: make sure you finish off a dangerous opponent first time around or he might make his second chance count."

Shearer laughed - a shallow grunt, devoid of humour or relish - and looked around again.

"Is that what you're doing right now then is it, Tommy?"

"Do you recognise where you are, Mick?"

A dead-end alleyway: sheer cliffs of brick on three sides; a broken pallet lying on the ground nearby. Shearer looked down at the chair: grey plastic with black metal legs. He sneered up at Tommy who carefully drew the sword from its wooden sheath and, in one swift fluid movement, made sure there would be no second chance coming Shearer's way.

5.

It's funny how things work out sometimes. I mean, I never harboured any ambitions to work for somebody like Tommy Stevens. I would go so far as to say it ranked high amongst the least likely things I imagined doing when the careers advisor asked what I wanted to do when I left school. But that's what happened.

I hated school; couldn't wait to get the fuck out of there the instant it became legally possible. It wasn't the learning stuff, or the mostly-pointless subjects that did it for me; it was the teachers. I doubt there's a place on earth where a larger gathering of useless, condescending arseholes can be found in one building. Except maybe Westminster, but that's not a fair fight. I left without qualifications to speak of and a bit of a bad attitude toward authority figures. I'd also managed to acquire a criminal record, thanks to a combination of stupidity and a couple of dodgy older mates.

The first strike was awarded for thieving some guy's bike from outside a pub one night. I was drunk and the aforementioned mates dared me - what more can I say? Unfortunately the area was covered by CCTV: operated by a wee guy in a control room, watching out for any bother and tipping off the cops if he saw anything untoward. I only got a couple of streets away from the scene before getting collared. Just my luck that one of those vigilant operators was on duty that night, instead of the type who likes to zoom in on women's arses and spends most of their time asleep or reading scud mags. A short bout of community service and a small fine followed.

The second award was much more serious and I'm not proud. These two mates loved a scrap: ran with a crew of football hooligans on match days; picked on unsuspecting innocents in-between-times. I've no idea why I joined in that night, but I did.

The lad was just stumbling home, a bit worse for drink, eating chips, bothering no-one. Well, no-one apart from Gary 'Gazza' Davidson and James 'Jimbo' Miller that is. They decided his ugly pus needed to make an acquaintance with their expensive trainers. For some unknown reason (I don't have the gall to blame it all on the drink), I decided he should also get to know my less-pricey, but far more hefty, Doc Martins. We battered that poor bastard to the ground and jumped all over him. He ate through a straw for the next six weeks and nearly died. I felt so ashamed, I couldn't look the lad's mum in the eye during the trial. As instigators and ringleaders, Gazza and Jimbo went down for two and four years respectively. They had form in relation to kicking fuck out of people for no good reason. I didn't, so I got away with a long bout of community service, a big fine and the warning that a third strike would see me moving in with the lads down Barlinnie way.

All of this made me a less-than-appealing candidate as far as prospective employers were concerned - the ones running legitimate businesses, at least. I spent three years on the dole, occasionally earning a few extra quid on building sites or delivering leaflets. Even the fast-food corporations proved to be fussy. Then Tommy Stevens came along.

I was slouching in front of the telly, some shit football match sending me into a coma, when the letterbox rattled. I opened the door to find The Stickman standing there, his back to me, leaning on his eponymous accessory. He swivelled on his good heel with surprising grace.

"Alright, Ross?"

"Eh, aye. Can I help you with something, Mr Stevens? You here to see my mum?"

Some people appear to have command over the sweat glands and heart rate of others, urging both to respond profusely in their presence. He was one of them.

"Naw, it's you I've come to see, son. Can you drive?"

He fixed me with that reptilian gaze and I was back at my mum's side, cowering.

"Aye, but I've not got a car at the minute. Can't afford one. Not got a job."

My mum provided the money for lessons the previous year, in a desperate bid to increase my employability. I'm pretty sure it was also in the hope that it might get me out of her house. But - just like me - it didn't work.

"Ok, that's fine. I'll supply the job and the motor. Come down to my garage at nine tomorrow morning and remember to bring your licence with you," he said, handing me a business card with the address on it. "Wear something half-smart and don't be late."

As he started to walk off down the path, I didn't know how to react; what to say. Part of me wanted to tell him to ram it, that working for someone like him was only ever going to turn out bad in the end, but a bigger part of me found the idea of working for a genuine gangster a genuine thrill. In truth, given my circumstances, I wouldn't be getting a better offer any time soon ... or ever. Even so, I should have questioned him; asked why he'd turned up at my door, out of the blue, with the offer of a job. Why me? Why now?

But I did not, could not ... dared not. Not yet, at least. Not right then.

"Ok, thanks, Mr Stevens. I'll see you at nine sharp."

Without stopping he glanced back.

"Call me Tommy."

I closed the door and stood there holding the handle. Shocked and stunned. Excited. Shitting myself.

The devil just came calling and I'd sold him my soul in return for a job as his chauffeur.

6.

It turned out Wee Baz had a surname – Turnbull. He was next.

Paul knew a guy, who knew a guy, who worked with Turnbull on building sites. In the last few months he'd been more occupied by tasks allocated by The Boss than he had been by labouring. However, according to Paul's source, Wee Baz was back making an honest living again - on a set of posh flats out Bearsden way. The brothers hatched their plan and drove out to the north-west of the city.

The site was not long under way. Great piles of materials stood, waiting to be meshed together to form a coherent living-space for the wealthy. Various vehicles, cement mixers, and other equipment required to complete the meshing together, kept the materials company.

A security fence topped with razor wire enclosed the site, adorned with signs promising any potential interlopers that they could expect bad-tempered, four-legged company if they dared to cross it. One of those bog-standard temporary lodgings you get on building sites appeared to house the canine defender and its masters.

After a couple of nights they got a good handle on the routine the security team followed and, thankfully, there was only one dog to consider. A substantial Doberman Pinscher mind you – one with those pointed ears sticking up like horns, making it look as if it had been spawned in Hades.

Wee Baz Turnbull seemed like a model employee. Turned up on time, worked his arse off during the shift, and left when the site closed for the night. He was bigger than Tommy remembered him to be and, judging by some of the feats of strength they watched him perform, someone to be very wary of. They'd not be taking any chances with this guy.

After three nights, the brothers were ready to make their move. As Wee Baz left the site and ambled down the street toward the train station, Tommy followed in the van. Paul waited behind a tree on the route they knew the big fellow would take. It was quiet; dark, save for the street lights; not much traffic about. Just as they hoped it would be.

As Turnbull passed by, Paul stepped out from his hiding place. The big man seemed to sense the sudden presence behind him and made to turn. In a flash, Paul plunged the needle into his neck. As Turnbull's legs gave way beneath him, Paul grabbed him under the armpits and dragged him to the back of the van as Tommy pulled up alongside the kerb. He bundled the torpid giant into the back, shut the doors and joined Tommy in the cab.

Slick and painless.

So far.

"Ok, bro', that's the first part done. Let's go."

At about two in the morning, they approached the fence on the southern side of the site. The guard and Daisy the Doberman (yet more obligatory nickname irony) would be round in the next few minutes. Paul used heavy cutters to make a hole in the fence, peeling back the mesh to form a makeshift door. Tommy stooped and went through first, making his way across to a substantial pile of bricks where he hunkered down. Paul came through after him and switched on his torch. The response to the beam of light cutting through the gloom was immediate.

Daisy started barking, straining at the leash of her handler, urging him to let her go chew on some interloping balls.

"Who's there? You better get yourself to fuck, mate, or

I'll set the dog on you."

Paul began to run and the guard let the dog off the leash.

"I warned you, mate. Go on girl, go get the thieving bastard!"

Both brothers could tell by the tone of his voice that this was a moment he'd been praying for since the day he started security work. A chance to see his prize pooch in action; doing what he'd trained her to do - but this time for real. No padded suit, no leather gauntlets, no muzzle, just razor-sharp teeth versus unprotected flesh.

The dog flew after Paul who stopped, turned off his torch and squatted down. As the slavering, snarling beast reached him and lunged, he stood up and enclosed the dog's head in a tarpaulin and wrestled it to the ground. It may have been a big strong dog, but it was no match for Paul. He yanked and hauled at the covering until the mutt was bound up like a steam pudding and it stopped struggling, whimpering in submission.

The handler lumbered after Daisy; not in the best of shape physically and a few years past his prime. He heard the muffled cries of his beloved companion and stopped. Right in line with Tommy's pile of bricks. Tommy walked up behind the guard and pushed the gun into the back of his neck.

"Don't turn around. Put this blindfold on, then put your hands behind your back. If you do as I say, you'll not get hurt. Understand?"

The man nodded. "What have you done to Daisy?"

"Don't worry about the dog, she'll be fine as well — assuming you don't give me any cause to change my plans."

"No, no, I'll do as you ask, mate. Just don't hurt the dog, please," said the guard, his sudden reclassification of the dog from deadly killer to helpless victim amusing Tommy.

With the blindfold on and his hands tied, Tommy

ushered the guard toward a portable toilet. He completed the job with a gag, pushed him inside, and secured the door with a padlock.

"Keep quiet and stay put."

Meanwhile, Paul sedated the dog and put it in the adjacent portable toilet.

As the fog in Wee Baz Turnbull's head began to clear, he could feel the wind whipping around his face. Head pounding, a whirlpool of nausea and bile skulked in his gut, threatening to rise to the surface. What the hell just happened? He shook his head, hoping it might knock the lenses in his eyes into focus. It didn't have the desired effect.

"Hello, Baz. Nice to see you again, mate."

The voice was other-worldly but familiar, for some reason.

"How's your head? I bet it's burling, eh?"

Baz shook his head again; this time he could see the outline of two people. Still blurred, but definitely two humanoid forms. One of them seemed to be speaking to him; knew his name. He wondered if he might be experiencing one of those alien abductions he'd heard about. He always thought they were bullshit, cooked up by geeks and deluded losers, but…maybe not? Maybe he was wrong and ET did take prisoners after all.

"So was mine, by the way. After you and the rest of the boys did your wee fandango on it."

Recognition and reason were creeping back through the drug-addled mist shrouding his thoughts. Baz definitely knew this guy. Definitely. And he was definitely not ET. He wanted to speak, but his tongue wouldn't move as instructed or required in terms of making sense.

"Still, I'm not bitter," said whoever-it-was-that-wasn't-ET.

The mist rolled back for a brief instant: Tommy 'Stickman' Stevens.

"Nah, that's a lie. I am bitter ... and pissed off, Baz. Really, really hacked off about the beating and even more pissed off about the knee-capping. I imagine you would be too if our places were reversed.

"Look, I know you were only doing what The Boss asked you to do. You just did what a good soldier is supposed to: you followed orders. However, when all is said and done, I can't just let that pass; can't just allow you to get away with it. I didn't let Mick get away with it, so, fair's fair."

The mist rolled back again and Baz could see he was perched above a deep hole in the ground – one of the excavations to be used as a foundation pile. He looked up at Tommy as The Stickman drew his sword from its sheath. A flash of steel in the moonlight and it was all over. Tommy pushed Baz into the hole with his foot. He and Paul then added a thin layer of soil. Just enough to cover him; to conceal him from the concrete pourers on the off-chance they looked into the hole before filling it. They needn't have bothered.

When the early shift arrived, the guard and Daisy were discovered and liberated. A quick inventory revealed no obvious theft, and no signs of break-in on any other parts of the site apart from the hole cut in the fence. It was baffling. Still, no harm done. Apart from the guard's shattered nerves and Daisy's rather more subdued manner, there was nothing to stop work continuing as normal.

Several weeks later, Wee Baz Turnbull's mother reported him missing but he was never seen again.

Two down, three to go.

7.

At eight forty-five in the morning I stood on the forecourt of 'Stevens Bros Auto Repair' and asked myself what the hell I thought I was doing. The garage was nothing special. Just another backstreet cut-and-shut shop with a faded sign, a single grimy window and a row of four metal shutters pulled down across the front of its maintenance bays. There were no signs of anyone being home.

The car sitting on the tarmac out in front of this unremarkable façade was, in every way, out of place. A gleaming, black, three-litre Audi A8; the paintwork so lustrous it looked like you could dip a quill in it and start writing. And I was going to be driving it! I mean, I'd only been driving for a year and the most powerful machine I'd taken full, unsupervised control of was a 1.6 Ford Focus. The flutter of butterflies I'd experienced on the bus journey down here became a churning tempest in my gut.

It was cold but bright; a few clouds scudding across the sky, driven by a brisk wind. What passed for a good day round these parts. Weather-wise, at least. I looked at the beautifully burnished lump of metal and realised it must have been sitting out there all night, unattended. And yet no-one in this poor, run-down, notorious part of town dared lay a finger on it. The licence plate read TS1 and it was sitting outside Stevens Bros Auto Repair. Everyone around there knew whose car it was and what would happen to them if they considered going within a few feet of it without the owner's express consent. I, too, resisted the temptation to approach it; I sat down on the retaining wall and waited.

At one minute before nine, a silver VW Golf GTi pulled into the forecourt and stopped alongside the Audi.

A brutish-looking guy I didn't recognise got out from behind the wheel and walked around to open the passenger-side door. Tommy Stevens swivelled in his seat, lifted his bad leg out over the running board and stood up, using his stick and the door for support. At the same time, the back door opened and the vision that is Victoria Stevens climbed out. The golden waterfall had been bobbed and augmented with a streak of pink but it didn't detract from her looks one bit as far as I was concerned.

I may have gasped.

Despite my enthusiasm regarding her attendance, she didn't look too enamoured to be there. She closed her door at the same instant as the brute did the same for Tommy, who moved toward me as I stood up.

"Ross, glad to see you're on time. A good start. Can't abide lateness. Remember that, son, and we'll get along just fine."

He turned to the brute.

"Ralph, go open up and put the kettle on will you, there's a good lad," he said, tossing a set of keys through the air which Ralph caught with aplomb, one-handed.

"Would have made a good cricketer that one, so he would. Don't you think?"

The smile revealed his once-crumbling row of headstones had received a rather swanky dental makeover. Hardly surprising, given the improvements in his financial situation in the intervening years. It helped soften him a little, compared to how I remembered him. Took away a touch of reptile; added back a dash of human being.

"Aye, I suppose so, not that I know anything about cricket mind you," I said.

My voice sounded tinny, hollow, like a Second World War radio broadcast. Victoria looked even less impressed. Not that I got a good look at her, as I was trying so hard not to make it obvious to all concerned how attractive I found her.

"Ross: this is Victoria, my daughter. Vicki, this is

Ross."

I nodded and extended my hand. She made a facial gesture I would place somewhere between contempt and apathy, before limply reciprocating. A wet fish of a handshake; that fish being an electric eel as far as I was concerned. I'd never known a girl affect me like this. It was exhilarating.

"Come on into the office, we'll get a brew and discuss this job I've got for you."

"Ok, that sounds grand," I said.

The office was what you'd expect of a back-street garage: functional, cluttered, masculine, a bit grimy. A calendar featuring an array of topless women hung on the wall; its secondary function being to let the owner know what day of the month it was.

"Milk or sugar?" asked Ralph.

"Just milk, ta," I said.

The tea was plonked down in front of me with what appeared to be a degree of resentment, slopping out onto the desk top. I didn't blame him, really. If I'd been asked to make a wee scrote like me a cup of tea, I might have felt a bit put out too. The teas for Tommy and Vicki were delivered with more care.

There were only three seats, so Ralph drew the short straw again and leant against the counter-top the kettle stood on. Yet more annoyance inflicted by yours truly. I didn't like making an enemy so soon. I liked the idea of making an enemy of this guy so soon even less; regardless of whether it was my fault or not.

"Did you remember your driving licence? I need it to put you on the insurance," said Tommy.

"Aye," I said, handing it over. "Will I be driving the Audi, by the way?"

Ralph spluttered tea, while Tommy broke out his new and improved gnashers.

"Eh, naw, wee man, you won't be driving the Audi, *by the way*. That's a sixty grand motor. You'll be driving the

37

Golf."

At this, Vicki produced a vicious scowl and tutted.

"What?" asked Tommy.

She shook her head and folded her arms, an expensive-looking smartphone gripped in her right hand.

"What's the problem, Vicki?"

There was steel in his voice; menace; a tone that indicated he'd hold no truck with dissent. And she recognised it.

"Nothing."

The mobile phone received a furious, two-thumbed pounding - no doubt a bitchy text or a Facebook update informing the world what a pair of pricks her father and I were.

"Good. Now, Ross, despite my daughter's display of bad manners, you're going to be her driver. She doesn't have a driving licence and I don't have the time or inclination to go shopping as often as she does. Just go where she asks you to take her and make sure she gets home safe from those bloody night clubs she's so fond of. Ok?"

My mind jumped back to that night a year ago: the desire, the giddy excitement, the humiliation. I wondered if she recognised me - but that was stupid. Being gawped at by lascivious, drunken youths would be a nightly occurrence for her. I imagined ripping the piss out of them with her mates would be just as common. I was nobody; a stupid, wee boy being asked to run her around town when she'd much rather have some hunky older man do the job.

"Aye, that sounds fine, Mr Stevens. Where should I take the car at the end of a shift?"

She huffed and took a slurp of her tea. Tommy shot her a look.

"You take it home, son. It's your company car, so to speak."

"Oh, right. What about petrol?"

"Here's some cash to get you started. Just get a receipt

every time you fill up, and me or Ralph will square you up when you collect your wages – which will be every Friday, by the way, down here at the garage."

He handed over a hundred pounds in tens and twenties. Stunned, I couldn't believe my luck. All the tension and misgivings I'd felt about working for The Stickman vanished as I pocketed the money. I wasn't working for him, I was working for her. A slave to the goddess, transporting her wherever she desired in her Teutonic steel chariot.

"Thanks, Mr Stevens."

"Oh, and here's a mobile for you to use. It's got Ralph, Vicki and my numbers in it. It's also got my brother Paul's – just in case you can't reach us - but only use that in a proper emergency. Understood?"

"Ok, Mr Stevens."

"Right then, that's settled. Ralph, give the laddie the keys. And Ross, call me Tommy, son. It's good you're showing respect but you're on the team now. Start as we mean to go on. Know what I mean?

"Ok, me and Ralph need to shoot the craw. You two wait here for wee Danny to come in. He should be here any time. When he does get here, you can do what you like. The world is your oyster and all that. I'll see you later on, Vicki. Play nice."

He leaned over, pecked her on the cheek, and he and Ralph left.

As soon as the door of the Audi closed, out on the forecourt, she started on me.

"Aye, that sounds fine Mr Stevens, thank you, Mr Stevens, can I take my tongue out of your ring-piece now, Mr Stevens," she said, in a sneering impersonation straight from the playground. It didn't matter. Every atom of my being buzzed with lust.

"You better get something straight, Ross. I don't need a driver and I didn't want a driver. It's just my dad's way of controlling me; keeping tabs on my movements. He'll be wanting you to grass me up; tell him where I've been; what I've been up to. But I'm warning you: if you grass on me I'll make your life a living hell. Do you understand?"

I just shrugged and nodded. "Aye, fine. I'm not a grass."

"Aye, well, we'll see. Right, there's wee Danny the fanny. Let's get the fuck out of this dump before he decides to talk to me. I can't stand that little wanker."

She stalked out of the office, blanking the fanny's attempts to greet her, and got into the back of the Golf. I followed after her: the loyal servant; lapdog - and loving it. I got behind the wheel; adjusted the driving position; put the key in the ignition.

"Where to?"

"The Fort."

The disdain oozed from her.

The phone received more opposable punishment.

I put the car into first and felt the vibrations of the engine through my foot; heard the growling note of approval as I pressed down on the accelerator.

I'd never felt a high like it.

8.

Gus Bowman suspected Tommy Stevens to be behind the killing of Mick Shearer but, just like the police, he couldn't prove it. Now, it seemed, Baz Turnbull had vanished. He cursed himself for failing to inflict a more conclusive punishment upon his one-time protégée. Tommy showed so much promise and would have made a great lieutenant, but the greedy bastard couldn't keep his fingers out of Gus' cookie jar. He liked Tommy that's why he only crippled him. But, instead of gratitude, all he got in return was fuss; disruption; interference with his business. That would be the last time he showed leniency when dealing with transgressors. Playing the nice guy didn't suit him; people didn't appreciate it; take it in the spirit intended.

"Rab, when did you last speak to Baz?"

"No' sure, Boss. Last week I think. He said he was going to work up in Bearsden on some building site."

"Right, well, he might just be off sunning himself somewhere in the Med, but I think we both know that our friend The Stickman must have paid him a visit."

Rab looked at Jimmy and they both nodded.

"I also think he'll be looking to settle his scores with you two soon, so let's make a pre-emptive strike. Get a couple of the lads and take Mr Stevens for a wee swim in the Clyde. Only, make sure he's wearing something heavy round his ankles when he jumps in. I don't ever want to hear from that lanky streak of piss again. Got it?"

"Yes, Boss."

Sweeney and McLean left to gather their army.

Gus Bowman sat down in his leather chair, swivelled to face the floor-to-ceiling windows of his office. The view across Glasgow from up on the fifteenth floor never failed to inspire him. Dark, menacing clouds gathered off to the west, while unfamiliar blue sky over the city itself seemed to tremble as they advanced. People scurried or sauntered in the streets below: oblivious, carefree, weighed down, tormented, ecstatic, miserable. A kaleidoscope of emotions, motivations, purpose and goals at work in the populace of Scotland's biggest city. But only one thing occupied the mind and emotions of The Boss: Tommy Stevens.

"Where's he most likely to be hanging about?" asked Rab Sweeney.

"No' that sure, mate. Let's try his ma's house, The Boss gave me the address," said Jimmy McLean.

Jimmy didn't know who'd used the van last but, whatever they'd been up to, they might have had the decency to clean up after themselves.

"Jesus wept, Jimmy. It smells like a hoor's drawers in here!" said Billy McNab.

"Aye, it's rank, but we've no time to be fannying about cleaning it out. You'll just need to get used to it."

"My fucking eyes are bleeding here, mate. Get used to it?" whined Geordie Hill, known to them all as Benny.

"Look, stop fucking moaning, Benny. There's fuck all I can do about it. Try breathing through your mouth or something."

The four of them squeezed into the front of the van, with barely enough room to breathe, so perhaps the stench would be moot.

It wasn't.

All the way to their destination, the men coughed, whinged and carped about being cooped up in their repellent vehicle.

The Stevens' family home was an unremarkable, three-bedroomed, two-storey, 1950's council house. The cracked, off-white render looking as if someone had drawn lines on it with a pen; the window frames in need of replacement; the roof in need of slight repair here and there. A tall, unkempt hedge surrounded the property; an empty gap indicating the gate was no longer around to hinder access from the pavement to the front path.

The four men waited in the van, much to Benny Hill's chagrin.

"Do we need to sit in here, Jimmy?"

"Look, will you give it a fucking rest, Benny. You've done nothing but moan your face off since you sat down. I told you, there's sweet fuck all I can do about the smell. We all know it's fucking bogging without you reminding us every two minutes, so just get on with it. Ok?"

Benny huffed; rolled his eyes. He tried to sit back in the seat but the combined bulk of Sweeney and McNab spread out when he sat forward and there was no shifting them again. Benny was by far the smallest of the trio, even if he was far from slight. The three men shuffled, shifted against each other, feeling awkward, enclosed, too close. Jimmy McLean tutted, returned his eyes to the house.

Sweeney let rip with an enormous, noxious fart. The other three decanted into the street, laughing, choking and hurling abuse back at him regarding his parentage, eating habits and personal hygiene. As they stood there, McLean became aware of movement at the front of the Stevens' house. Paul Stevens walked out of the front door and up the garden path. When he saw the van and its trio of disgorged passengers, he stopped.

McLean locked eyes with the younger Stevens brother. Not the main prize, but he could prove to be useful bait.

"Stevens, where's that lanky cripple of a brother of yours?"

Paul put out his cigarette and walked toward McLean. This was his lucky day: the next name on Tommy's hit list just rolled up outside his front door. By rights he should wait for his brother to join him, to allow him the pleasure of his revenge, but there was no time like the present - couldn't look a gift horse in the mouth, etc. Tommy wasn't around, and this was in the days when mobile phones were far from the ubiquitous items they are now. Contacting him wouldn't have been easy or quick enough to ensure he got there in timely fashion. It might be three against one, but Paul still fancied his chances.

"Watch your mouth, McLean. What the fuck is it to you where Tommy is?"

"Paulo, Paulo, Paulo, you know fine well The Boss needs to have a wee chat with Tommy – thinks he might have had something to do with Mick Shearer's death and Wee Baz's disappearance. The Boss isn't too chuffed about that; wants to check with Tommy, see if it's true or not."

The three men lined up almost shoulder to shoulder as Paul advanced. He failed to notice Rab Sweeney slip out of the front seat and behind the van.

Paul increased his pace, closing the gap with a rapidity that caught the three men by surprise. He head-butted McLean with such force that his nose shattered and he folded like a Swiss Army knife. Almost in the same movement, he delivered a crashing roundhouse kick to Hill's temple, sending him sideways and down. McNab, by far the biggest of the three men, rugby-tackled him to the ground; landing on top of him, punching and forearm-smashing as he tried to gain the advantage. Paul wriggled and twisted, deflecting blows with his arms, before rolling the big man over to find himself on top. He let his own pummelling commence.

The bat connected with the side of Paul's head with considerable force, leaving him sprawled on top of McNab, unconscious. Rab Sweeney stood, surveying the carnage. It happened so quickly, he'd had no time to get in before Paul wreaked havoc on his companions. All four of the other men in the street lay unconscious or semi-conscious. Three of them bleeding. He dragged Paul around to the back of the van and manhandled him in before helping the now-recovering Hill and McNab back to their feet. All three of them managed to manoeuvre the insensible McLean into the front seat.

"Ok, let's get out of here before someone calls the cops. We need to have a word with The Boss and see what he wants to do about this," said Sweeney, taking temporary charge. "I think I know what he's going to say, mind you, but let's just make sure."

The other two concurred as they drove off.

"Tommy?"

"Aye, is that you, Paul?"

"Aye, listen, bro', I've fucked up. The Boss sent a team around and ..."

The line went dead. Tommy dropped the phone back onto the cradle and stood looking at it, confused by the curtailed message, the tone of his brother's voice. The Boss sent a team round? That did not sound like a good thing.

The phone rang again.

"Paul? What the ..."

"Shut the fuck up, Tommy, and listen to me. I don't take kindly to those who cross me, but you know that only too well. At least, I thought you did. Get down to the warehouse; I need a wee chat with you about Mick Shearer and Baz Turnbull."

"Gus? You think I still need to do what you tell me?"

"Oh, I reckon you'll do as I say, you cheeky bastard – if you ever want to see your brother again. Be there at eleven pm."

"You do realise I'm going to kill you, Gus?"

Laughter rolled down the line before the connection was cut.

Tommy took some time to prepare. He called in his cousins Steve and Frank: back-up if things got hairy. He got into his car around ten, wanting to make sure he'd be there in plenty of time. The boys would follow in a separate vehicle.

The warehouse sat on the riverside, anonymous,

blending in. Gus Bowman used it for storing all manner of merchandise; holding clandestine meetings; delivering punishments. The dull, grey water of the River Clyde carried a multitude of sins on its way past this place. It held a few dark secrets in its depths as well, and Tommy knew Bowman fully intended to add him to its tally tonight. The Boss was going to be disappointed, though.

Tommy knew the site well. He parked a few streets away, aiming for the element of surprise; to arrive without being noticed - until it was too late for Gus to do anything about it.

The cloudy sky amplified the darkness. As he got out of his car, it began to rain. This suited him fine. Tommy liked the rain. Living in the west of Scotland, the copious precipitation gave him plenty of chances to enjoy it. Liking it meant he didn't let it affect his judgement or mood. Another small advantage. His cousins pulled up behind him, as arranged earlier. He briefed them on how he wanted them to handle it.

Tommy walked with purpose, the bad leg not allowed to hinder his progress. Sure, it ached and protested - but it could shut the fuck up for now, there would be time enough later for taking notice of pain. He stopped on the corner, scanning the front of the building for sentries. Billy McNab stood smoking by the side entrance, collar turned up, moving from foot-to-foot to ward off the chill. He'd be first then. Tommy didn't mind about the running order any more. Bowman had forced his hand – what would be, would be.

Tommy worked his way around the back of the building via a couple of alleys and yards, keeping close to the buildings as much as he could. He walked up the side passage of the warehouse, staying in the shadows, letting his feet fall with as little sound as possible. McNab was facing away from him, almost certainly expecting Tommy to arrive in front of the building by car. Nobody defied The Boss; it was incomprehensible that Tommy would do anything other than fold; turn up with his tail between his legs and take his punishment. That mind-set would give him the edge he needed. That, and the tempered steel sheathed within his walking stick.

Tommy eased the sword free, advanced the last few yards and tapped McNab on the shoulder with it. The big man turned. The sword drove up and through him, giving him no time to respond, defend himself, call out. Tommy retracted the blade and McNab fell to his knees then thumped onto his face; dead before he could feel the tarmac against his cheek.

Tommy rapped on the metal door McNab had been guarding, then pressed up against the wall beside it. Geordie Hill, the one folk liked to call Benny, stepped into the passageway. He looked down at his fallen comrade, frowned, looked up and to his left in time to see the blade glint as it connected with his neck. Tommy heard the commotion begin inside as the other occupants of the warehouse realised something was amiss. Muffled shouts; Bowman's voice the one delivering the instructions.

Slinking back along the wall, Tommy crouched down behind a collection of oil barrels, crates and pallets about twenty metres from the doorway. His knee protested. He did his best to ignore it.

Jimmy McLean was first to emerge, with much more caution than Hill, carrying a gun.

"Tommy, I know you're out here, man. You better give yourself up now or Paul won't be worrying about his old age pension anymore."

McLean crept forward, tension crackling from him like a static charge. He didn't look entirely at ease with the idea of using a firearm. This wasn't The Bronx; guns were a last resort, rarely used. As a rule, McLean much preferred using his fists – they'd served him well so far.

Tommy felt calm, at one with himself and what he needed to do.

McLean advanced, tentative, attempting to sound in

control of his nerves but fooling no-one.

"Tommy, give yourself up, this is only going to end one way."

Tommy stood up from behind the barrels and brought the sword down on McLean's wrist, severing his hand. It fell to the ground still gripping the gun.

"You're absolutely right, Jimmy. It is," said Tommy, as he swept the blade across the back of McLean's knees.

The big man began screaming in a way Tommy had never experienced before or since. The pain of his own knee-capping shuddered through him but he felt no pity for McLean; no remorse. This was right; required; inevitable.

Tommy prised the gun from McLean's disembodied mitt, tucked it into his waistband and moved toward the open doorway, light spilling into the darkness of the passageway. He could hear Bowman shouting from somewhere inside.

"Jimmy? You ok, man?"

McLean tried to muster some sort of coherent response but only managed to groan, his vocal chords shot, the pain and blood loss overwhelming him.

"Jimmy?" repeated Bowman. "Tommy? You better stop now while you and your brother are still breathing. Give yourself up and I'll let Paul go. Otherwise, you're both going to endure the worst night of your lives. Do you hear me, Tommy?"

"How about I make you an offer, Gus? How about you let Paul go right now and I won't come in there and kill you and Sweeney?"

The same laugh as on the phone earlier.

"Come ahead you wanker, do your worst!" shouted Rab Sweeney.

Tommy lay on the ground and rolled through the doorway. A shot flew over him, Sweeney failing to predict how low down he'd be; aiming as if he'd walked in upright. Tommy returned fire, crawling at pace toward some cover behind a stack of boxes and pallets. His knee made more protests. He continued to pretend not to hear them.

Another shot whizzed overhead, ricocheting off a beam somewhere behind him.

"Paul? Are you ok, mate?"

No response. Tommy glanced out from his hiding place. Another bullet made a bid to embed itself in him but failed in its mission. Just.

Only a glimpse, but it was enough. Paul, hanging from a rope in the middle of the building: blood dripping, puddling beneath him, apparently already dead.

White noise filled his ears; grief sliced through him, keener than the blade he carried. But rage would be Tommy's enemy. Paul deserved revenge. Tommy needed calm, control, clear thought processes. He moved to the other end of the boxes; looked out again. Sweeney and Bowman took cover behind a stack of boxes side by side, both armed.

"Tommy, it's over. Give yourself up and I'll make it quick and painless."

"Like you did for Paul?"

"He was nearly as stubborn as you, Tommy. But it's your fault he's dead, not mine. You couldn't keep your hands off my stuff, then when I gave you a wee rap across the knee, you decided to try and wipe out my team. Paul's death is just an unfortunate by-product of your greed, your arrogance. Do us all a favour, just give it up."

Tommy crept across a gap between stacks of boxes. The two men were looking about, peeking out from behind their hiding place, trying to locate him by where his voice was coming from. Tommy aimed through a pallet, fired a single shot. Sweeney's head burst like a ripe tomato, showering Bowman with the contents of his skull. Tommy was impressed by how unruffled Bowman seemed. He wiped some of the viscera and blood from his face before scrambling away from the boxes and behind another set of pallets. Tommy fired again but missed.

One more to go.

"Tommy, you need to know there are more of my lads on the way. You're not getting out of here alive, I will guarantee you that."

"What makes you think *I* came here by myself, Gus?"

Bowman experienced his first moment of doubt. He'd not thought about whether Tommy would bring anyone else. He assumed Tommy was a lone wolf; a rebel without a cause; just an upstart with ideas and ambitions way above and beyond his actual capabilities. Sure, there was the brother, but he'd been dealt with already. Who else would there be? Five against one should have been plenty – particularly when the one concerned used a stick to help him walk. Had he underestimated him? He didn't get the time to ponder this any further. As he sat with his back to the pallets and boxes he'd dived behind, Tommy doubled back on himself and sneaked round Bowman's blind side. The gun barrel pressed into the back of The Boss's neck and he knew it was time.

"Drop the shooter, Gus."

The gangster complied.

"Tommy, you need to understand. It's business. I can't have ..."

"Shut the fuck up, Gus, and get on your feet."

Bowman stood and turned to face Tommy. The sword came up to rest under his chin.

"You thought you could cripple me for taking a tiny wee bit of gear. That was bad form on your part, but my main gripe lay with the boys who did it: your sheep. I wasn't sure whether I should tackle you directly, but you've gone and killed Paul, so this is it. The end."

Tommy shot Bowman in the knee. He fell to the floor writhing in agony.

"Not nice is it, Gus?"

"This isn't over, Tommy. This isn't how this ends, you arrogant prick."

The desperation of a man who knows he's defeated. So

often the one delivering, now the one on the receiving end.

"Oh, I think you'll find it is, Gus."

Tommy pushed the sword into Bowman's abdomen. Slowly, and with relish. Bowman grabbed at the blade, trying in vain to prevent it piercing him, lacerating his hands as Tommy twisted the sword before withdrawing it. Blood rushed from his wounds, filling his oesophagus, choking and drowning him.

The Boss is dead.

Long live The Boss.

Tommy stood back, his attention turning to Paul. He rushed toward his brother, cutting him free, catching him as he fell. Tommy's knee finally gave up the ghost. He collapsed in a heap, holding his sibling tight; tears of grief, guilt and frustration flowing.

"Why didn't you wait for me, Paul?" he said to the world. "Why?"

It would be futile but he laid Paul flat, checked his pulse. Nothing. Tommy began CPR; had to do something, no matter how pointless it might be.

He looked up as Steve and Frank came into the warehouse.

"Holy fuck, Tommy, what happened?" said Steve.

"That bastard Bowman strung Paul up, so I killed him," replied Tommy, still trying to revive his brother. The first bout of mouth-to-mouth brought Paul, coughing, back into the world.

"Jesus Christ! Paul, you're going to be alright, mate. Hang in there, I'll get you to a hospital. Frank, Steve, help me get him to the car."

The cousins rushed forward, lifting Paul between them, heading for the car they'd left out front as Tommy re-sheathed his sword and hobbled after his three relatives. As he entered the side passageway again, Jimmy McLean's low moaning re-ignited his ire. Tommy pulled out the sword; finished the last of The Boss's team off. No second chances, no loose ends. Start as he meant to go on.

The three of them would return to clear up this mess once he'd ensconced Paul in the care of Glasgow's finest medical professionals.

9.

I sat in the car waiting for Vicki. She'd been a total bitch the entire way from the garage to the shopping centre. I toyed with the phone, looking at her number, thinking about how many lads would give their right nut to get a hold of that string of digits. I'd got it without trying - not from her, mind you, but that was being churlish. She told me she'd text when she wanted to be picked up again but, in the meantime, would I kindly fuck off and leave her alone. I did as she asked.

There was no denying how hard I'd fallen for her but, it would be fair to say, I was also a little deflated at the sheer vehemence of her contempt for me. Luckily, I was born an optimist. I felt confident I'd win her round - even if it took a while.

The phone rang. I juggled it in surprise, managing to avoid dropping it by the narrowest of margins.

"Hello?"

"Ross?"

"Aye."

"Tommy here. How's it going, son?"

"Eh, fine."

"How's Vicki?"

As predicted by the girl herself: Dad was on the phone, checking up on her, trying to get me to grass her up. Even though there was nothing to grass up... probably. The truth was, I didn't know precisely where she was. The whole 'going to the shops' thing might have been a ruse. For all I knew, she could have done a runner on me; off to sell her body for heroin or lying in a gutter off her face on drink. At ten o'clock in the morning this seemed unlikely but, even so, I really didn't know for sure.

It dawned on me that this dream job could very soon become a horror show of stress and egg-shell treading, if I couldn't find an acceptable balance between father and daughter - and fast.

"Aye, she's fine."

A short pause.

"She there?"

"Eh, naw, she's in the shops."

"Right, and where are you then?"

I wondered if someone set a fire underneath the car seat while I wasn't looking. Sweat began to form on my top lip. I shifted, all moisture in my mouth disappearing.

"In the car park at The Fort. She made me wait here, didn't want me trailing round the shops with her."

Another pause.

"Right. I should maybe have been a bit clearer with my instructions this morning, Ross. Vicki's my daughter and I love her but she can be a stubborn wee so and so. You don't let her out of your sight. Do you hear me?"

"Eh, aye, ok, Mr Steve ...Tommy. She *really* didn't want me to go into the Centre with her though."

"No, I'm sure she didn't, son. Look, I don't expect you to go into every bloody clothes shop she visits, but I need you to keep her in sight as much as you can. There are a few folk out there I'd rather she didn't bump into on her own. Do you know what I mean?"

I did know what he meant and I didn't feel at all at ease with having it pointed out to me. Who did he think I was - a cross between Kevin Costner and bloody Jason Statham?

"Tommy, you do realise I'm not a bodyguard or into martial arts or anything like that? I don't want to bullshit you as far as that sort of thing goes. I wouldn't want to let you down or see anything bad happen to Vicki."

The obvious, selfish truth was: although I really didn't want anything bad to happen to Vicki, I was much more concerned about bad things happening to me if she did come to any harm. It felt peculiar admitting a level of physical ineptitude to a guy like Tommy. I was never what anyone would have called a 'hard man' but I never got bullied either. I didn't scrap like a demon but had a few ding-dongs as I went through school and came out on top more than I got battered. I wondered if I might be signing my own P45, only a matter of hours into the job? Maybe I should have done what actors say you should always do at auditions. If the director asks you, "Can you fight?" you say, "Yes". You get the part, then you pay someone a fortune to give you a crash course in fighting.

"Listen, son, I know you're not Rambo. I didn't hire you for your brawn. I want someone with her that won't wade in without thinking; make things worse. You've got a phone with mine and Ralph's number's on it: the minute you suspect anything is wrong, you call one of us. Ok?"

"Aye, ok."

"The main thing I want you to do is stop her getting dodgy mini-cabs home from clubs or, worse still, stoating home on foot, pissed out of her head. I want you to help her with her bags, take her where she wants to go and casually, without her knowing it, keep an eye out for any bother. Do you get it now, son? Is that clear?"

"Totally, Tommy. That sounds fine."

I wondered if he was convinced because I sure as fuck wasn't. I wondered if I knew anyone who could teach me a few ninja death grips or the like. I considered whether I should get tooled up but I soon dismissed that idea. The law was coming down hard on anyone caught carrying a knife these days and if that became my third strike, I'd definitely be facing a stretch in jail.

"Good lad. Now, go into that Centre and track the silly wee madam down. Right?"

"Will do, Tommy. Cheers."

"Aye, see you later, Ross."

He rang off and I breathed out with force, tension spinning round the inside of the car like a mini typhoon. Now, to face the fearsome queen of my dreams.

She would be so happy to see me.

"What part of 'stay in the car and leave me the fuck alone' did you not understand, Ross?"

I shook my head, tried to stay calm. It's fine being abused by your boss's daughter; it's fine being abused by a woman you find incredibly attractive ... up to a point, then it becomes tiresome and you feel compelled to defend yourself.

"What?" she snapped.

"Nothing. Look, Vicki, I can't win here. You want me to fuck off; your dad wants me to keep you in sight."

"Oh, boohoo. I don't care about your problems, Ross. I also don't care what my dad says. If he phones and asks where I am, just lie. Tell him I'm in the toilet, a changing room, whatever, but I do not want you following me round like a wee dog, making notes on everything I'm up to. Got it?"

Something snapped.

"No, no I haven't '*got it*'! I don't need to put up with this shit. I never asked for this poxy job; your dad just gave it to me out of the blue. Why me? I've not got a fucking clue. If you don't want me driving for you, fine. I'll tell your dad it's not working out and I'll bugger off. I tell you what though, he'll just get someone else. If you think you can get away without him watching you, you're kidding yourself on."

She looked at me in a different way; didn't immediately slap me down. I felt my cheeks flush, regretting the level of anger in my voice.

"Ooh, touchy!" she said, raising her eyebrows and breaking out one of the first smiles I'd seen since I met her that morning.

"Aye, well. I'm just saying, likes," was my sheepish response.

She started to walk toward a coffee shop: one of those big corporate places that charge the equivalent of a month's rent for a latte. A latte that's so big it goes cold before you can get anywhere near finishing it and, even if you did, you'd be pissing like a racehorse for days. After a few paces she stopped and turned round.

"I thought you were supposed to be following me?" she said, opening her arms and raising her shoulders.

I shook my head, smiling, lust sweeping through me like a tidal surge. As I drew alongside her, she began to walk again.

"I've decided to let you buy me a coffee."

I was the kind of light-headed with excitement and desire which you think only exists in slushy novels and chick flicks. She was my queen again.

10.

Drew Fleming was at war with life. Aggression, violence and domination must have been in his bloodstream; part of his DNA. He couldn't blame any of it on a bad upbringing: his parents might not have been rich or well-educated but they had morals; took an interest in his life; provided a good example; expected better. Wherever this behaviour came from, it needed to be traced further back than their doorstep. Something inside him was broken and it couldn't be fixed by them, or anyone else.

Anne Fleming should never have married Drew. Life with him overflowed with disappointment. Physical threats became promises delivered, and when they failed to subjugate her, psychological oppression replaced fists and boots. Their romance started off as passionate, feisty, lustful, exciting. She fulfilled all the clichés required of her in falling for a handsome, charming brute who everyone told her to stay the hell away from. He intercepted and smashed all her other close relationships, leaving her dependent, adrift. Her solace was small and boy-shaped.

Ross.

It seemed so unnatural, given his wont for exerting his will by force, but Drew never laid a finger on Ross. The boy appeared incapable of lighting any kind of fire underneath his normally combustible father. Apple of his eye; could do no wrong - although this might have been stretching the reality. The fact that Drew spent little or no time interacting with the boy helped him avoid any loss of temper. Not really Drew's fault mind you - his criminal empire wouldn't run itself.

Anne knew Drew was a bit of a bad boy; had run-ins with the law now and again. It was only after they married that she came to realise how understated 'a bit of a bad boy' was. Drugs, protection, gambling and probably prostitution (he tried hard to stop her proving that one), all helped fund a lifestyle she could never enjoy through the ever-present fear of legal intervention or Drew's spoiling tactics. To the outside world, they had it all.

Until Tommy Stevens came along.

The affair started on a wet August afternoon while Ross attended nursery. Drew made it clear Anne should not socialise with any of the other mums. Such was his influence over her, she complied, withdrawing to a small café to sip tea and read a book until it was time to go and pick Ross up again. That day she sat staring out the window at the wooden decking, watching the rain hit the grooves in the wood, the water appearing to roll sideways to right and left simultaneously. Hypnotised; tuned out from the rest of human kind.

"Another lovely summer's day."

She looked up, glazed, only half aware of her surroundings. On a couch across the room a tall, slim guy, broadsheet newspaper spread across his lap, smiled at her. Despite the teeth exposed by the smile being in poor condition, she found the owner alluring; she would find it hard to express why to a third party. A man at ease with himself; giving the impression of cool relaxation rather than swagger or arrogance. Good looking, despite the teeth, she supposed; whatever that meant. Well dressed: a suit from a tailor rather than a high street shop and a pair of expensive-looking designer shoes. A stick with an ornate handle leaning against the couch.

"Yes, isn't it just," she replied, a strange warmth growing in her gut.

"What are you reading?"

She looked down at the book in her hands.

"It's *'Trainspotting'* by Irvine Welsh."

"Any good?"

"Aye, it's fantastic, actually. Really different; really

Scottish. Grim at times but funny too," gushed Anne.

"Aye, a couple of my pals have said I should read it but I've not got around to it yet."

"Oh, you won't be disappointed."

After this sudden burst of enthusiasm, a stilted silence descended. Anne sipped at her lukewarm but passable tea; Tommy fidgeted with his paper.

"I'm Tommy, by the way," he said.

"Anne."

"Nice to meet you, Anne."

She blushed; smiled a coy smile. The warmth spread.

Tommy was smitten.

Drew and Tommy knew each other: wary adversaries, respectful distances kept. Both men garnered reputations sufficient for the other to avoid out-and-out conflict if possible. They worked different areas of the city. Tommy concentrated on gambling, counterfeit goods, car ringing and money laundering through his legitimate businesses to provide his income. Drugs and whores were Drew's favoured nefarious business activities. Tommy would never have entered into a conversation with Anne, let alone have an affair with her, if he'd known her marital status from the outset.

Too late for that.

The inevitable day of reckoning came six months into their dalliance.

Drew, being the controlling and manipulative type that he was, found it too hard to trust his wife to be left to her own devices while his son painted every surface within reach and ate sand by the handful. One of his guys got dispatched to spy on Mrs Fleming. His job: to report back on any deviations from the strict instructions Drew issued to her with regard to socialising. The fury Drew felt when he learnt of Anne's actual whereabouts and the company she kept, while Ross took his first foray into organised education, threatened to cause him an embolism.

61

Tommy and Anne were ensconced in a small hotel a few streets away from the nursery. An unremarkable frontage, surrounded by residential properties and a few bed-and-breakfast places. It meant she was close enough to react to any emergency with the wee man but it may as well have been on a different planet as far as Anne was concerned. Those two hours in bed with Tommy, two or three times a week - depending on his schedule - made her feel whole again; like the part of her inner self that Drew stole, stamped on and discarded had been returned to her. Tommy's lovemaking skills were adequate; pleasant rather than mind-blowing. Occasionally he would surprise her but, on the whole, he was safe and predictable. It shouldn't have affected her so much, but it did. Tommy seemed to care about her; took his time trying to please her, even if his attempts often fell short of delivering orgasmic bliss. She liked making him feel good; she liked him full stop.

If she'd realised who he was when he first spoke to her, though, she would not have encouraged his advances.

The afternoon rain fell as if the clouds couldn't get rid of it quickly enough. Days like that always made the safe warmth of Tommy's arms, in a soft bed, all the more appealing. The hotel owner, Fergus Ryan, got to know them well. He guessed they were indulging in an affair but the extra income they brought in helped him overlook any religious or moral misgivings about providing a venue for their adulterous liaisons. As long as Anne wasn't getting paid, it wasn't any of his concern. What the tax man didn't see, the VAT man wouldn't lose any sleep over. When Drew asked him for their room number, Fergus needed to be persuaded to part with the information.

"Ricky, watch the door. Don't let anyone else in," said Drew to his substantially-built henchman.

Fergus lay on the floor, bleeding from the nose and mouth, left pinkie twisted at an abnormal angle.

Drew walked up the stairs to the first floor, along the characterless corridor to room number four. He stopped outside the door, listening. A murmur of voices, but no carnal grunting or moaning as far as he could tell. Stepping back, he let his boot connect just below the handle. The door gave way in a loud splintering of frame. Tommy rolled out of bed, naked. Anne screamed, her ample bare breasts exposed as she sat up.

"Drew! What the ..."

"Shut the fuck up, whore, I'll deal with you in a minute."

Pulling out a gun, Drew pointed it at Tommy as he advanced into the room.

"On your knees, Stevens. Hands behind your head."

Tommy did as instructed.

"Drew, please, don't ..."

"One more word from you, slut, and I'll shoot you in the face. Got it?"

The look in Drew's eyes reminded Anne of the worst night of her life; a different night where she'd almost died, when only luck and the intervention of his sister's boyfriend prevented Drew from drowning her in the swimming pool of their holiday villa. She got it. She got it all too well. This time, there would be no intervention. This time, he *would* kill her.

Drew pressed the gun against Tommy's forehead.

"I thought we had an understanding, Tommy. I thought you kept out of my way and, in return, I kept out of yours. Looks like I was wrong. I kept out of your way and, in return, you fucked my wife."

"Drew, I'm sorry mate. I had no idea she was your wife," said Tommy.

Drew smashed Tommy in the head with the gun, sending him to the floor in a heap, blood oozing from a deep gouge caused by the handle.

"We're not fucking mates, you wanker."

Anne screamed again. She thought about trying to help her lover but huddled back against the head-board instead when her husband pointed the gun at her. She pulled the sheet up to her chin, sobbing, waiting for the inevitable.

"You're also a fucking liar! How would you *not* know she was my wife? Everybody knows that bitch is mine."

Tommy tried to clear his head; refocus his vision; think how he was going to get out of this. Drew looked down at the prone figure, the scars on Tommy's shattered knee appearing very white against his hairy legs.

"Look, Drew, you don't need to do this. I didn't know who she was. Honestly, I didn't," said Tommy, hoping reason might be an option.

"Back on your knees, Stevens. I want to hear you beg me not to kill you."

Something in Tommy closed down the shutters when he heard this. He never begged. Reason wouldn't work here. He shot upwards, grabbing for the gun, driving his head into Drew's face as he rose. Drew dodged the head-butt enough to prevent a devastating impact but it still dropped him. Trying to twist toward Tommy as he fell, Drew let off a shot from the suppressed gun, the bullet embedding itself in the ceiling. Plaster rained down as the two men grappled with each other. Anne screamed again, diving out of the bed onto the floor.

After a couple of seconds she found the courage to peek over the top of the bed. To her horror, Drew gained the upper hand. He stood and put the gun against the side of Tommy's head once again.

"Right, Stevens, you bastard. If you're not going to beg, it's time to say your prayers."

Anne swung the stick with as much force as she could manage. It connected with the back of Drew's head where his neck joined his skull. A sickening crack accompanied the blow as Drew folded on top of Tommy without expletive or exclamation. Tommy wriggled out from under him, standing up; head pink with a mixture of plaster dust and blood, breathing heavily. Anne dropped the stick onto the bed, put her face in her hands, and wept.

Tommy stooped, felt for a pulse, put his ear on Drew's

chest.

"Fuck. I think he's dead."

Anne looked up, shock sweeping across her face, eyes wide like saucers.

"What? No, he can't be."

She climbed off the bed and checked Drew's pulse, put her ear to his chest, grabbed a mirror from the bedside table and put it in front of his mouth. A trickle of blood trickled out from one of his nostrils.

Tommy wasn't wrong.

"No, no, no, this can't be happening. Tommy, what are we going to do?"

Tommy started to get dressed. Whatever they were going to do, he'd be doing it with his trousers on.

Ricky Banks stood, blocking the entrance to the hotel, with arms folded; impassive. It was a pose he felt comfortable with, deploying it most evenings while working the door of Drew's club. He was the kind of bouncer nobody argued with. If he said you weren't getting in, you weren't getting in.

Fergus Ryan sat in his reception-desk chair, dabbing at his nose with a wad of tissue. The worst of the bleeding staunched, but his pride permanently dented. Nausea looped in his over-sized gut; his bald head thumped. One of his teeth throbbed, loosened by a punch. No doubt it would cost him a pretty fucking penny when his robbing bastard of a dentist came to look at it. His twisted finger sang with pain: a tuneless, high-pitched screech of a song. Not only that, but these minor injuries looked like being this pair's 'starter for ten'. They'd let him see their faces; made no attempt to cover their tracks. As the primary witness, it didn't bode well for his future. Dampness spread across his rather-too-tight shirt; adrenaline flooded his bloodstream; the nausea threatened to do more than loop.

Guilt also nagged at Fergus. It wasn't long into the

beating before he realised Drew must be Anne's cuckolded husband and he'd just sent the gun-toting, digit-mangling thug upstairs to do God-knows-what to her and Tommy – and him disabled, too. Drew hadn't left him with a lot of choice in the matter but it still didn't make him proud.

The commotion from the upper floor stilled. Ricky became restless; he wasn't sure whether to go check or stay put as instructed. It didn't take long for him to make his mind up.

"Help, help!" shouted Anne from upstairs.

Ricky bounded up the steps two and three at a time, showing a surprising turn of speed and agility for such a big man. He pulled open the fire door at the end of the corridor and took Tommy's stick full in the face as he did so. The big man fell to the floor, out cold, nose widened and flattened in the process.

Tommy made his way down to the lobby. The rotund hotel manager had the phone in his hand but put the receiver back on the cradle when Tommy gestured with his stick to do so.

"What are you going to do to me?" stammered Fergus.

"If you do exactly as I say? Nothing," replied Tommy.

Tommy lifted the phone and dialled.

"Steve? It's Tommy. I need you and Frank over here right away, there's been a bit of an incident."

"Right you are Tommy, what's up like?"

"Never mind the details, I'll fill you in when you get here. Bring the van and the cleaning kit. It's the Rosebridge Hotel in Giffnock. You know it?"

"Aye, we'll be with you in about an hour, cuz."

Tommy hung up, turned to Fergus.

"You got any booze?"

The hotelier nodded. "Malt?"

"Just the ticket, I think me and you need to have a wee chat, Fergus, don't you?"

Given the choice, Fergus would rather have given it a miss.

11.

An uneasy truce broke out between me and Vicki. She didn't exactly gush with enthusiasm or throw herself into my arms – if only – but she passed the time of day with me, polite, matter-of-fact, less bossy. Not sure I preferred that version.

Car journeys, shopping, a sandwich for one, watching her meet up with mates she hardly ever introduced me to, lots of sitting about. I almost took up reading again to relieve the boredom.

This mundanity didn't last long.

Friday morning, I tagged along behind her as she shopped. Vicki deigned to allow me this privilege now. As it happens, watching her phenomenal arse wiggle along in front of me was very much a privilege.

Vicki loved shopping; spending Tommy's money like water, turning hard cash into a plethora of superficial crap. I wondered if that's how Jesus would impress folk these days if he came back to perform a few miracles. I assumed it must've been Tommy's money as she didn't work. Unless traipsing round the shops could be called work. She did go every day, almost from nine until five, so maybe she considered it her job. Daddy's dirty money spent on a pile of shit she didn't need. No other person alive could have owned more clothes than this girl. I found it amusing and irritating in almost equal measure. The supply of money seemed endless. That's what made her behaviour so surprising.

The store wasn't overrun with customers, given it was a school day; outside any recognised holiday period; and, two weeks since most folks' pay days. It would have been fair to describe it as dead, which made what she did even less sensible. While she browsed I carried a few bags around for her, stood back a few feet, let her have some space. I certainly wasn't going to be any use to her as a fashion advisor. She walked past me. I felt something drop into one of the bags at my feet, so I glanced down. A red lace thong lay on top of the jeans she'd bought in the last place; still on its mini hanger, price tag still attached. I felt confusion clatter around inside my head, swiftly followed by fear at the realisation of what she was up to.

"Vicki," I hissed. "What the actual fuck?"

She smiled her most seductive smile, shook her head, fluttered her eyelashes, walked away.

I didn't know what to do. Should I go along with this nonsense? Should I put the thong back where she lifted it from, or maybe just hang it up on the nearest available rack?

She passed by again. Another item of lingerie dropped into the bag.

I tried to grab her but missed. She weaved between the shop fittings, the scent of mischief hanging in the air. Not a smell I took to. Not an aroma I imagined Tommy 'The Stickman' Stevens being over-fond of either.

She looked back at me.

"Come on, Ross. Nothing I want in here. Let's go."

I glared at her, brow more furrowed than a recently-ploughed wheat field. Looking her up and down, I realised she had trainers on today, as opposed to the heels of the previous couple of days. The mad bint planned this, she'd come prepared; we were going to have to leg it.

As we approached the entrance lobby my bottle almost crashed but she must have sensed my reticence. She looped her arm through mine and chivvied me along, right out the doors. As the alarm sounded she burst into a run. I had no other option than to follow suit, as a lumbering security guy who looked about seventy (years old *and* stones in weight) attempted to intercept us.

The shop doors opened out onto Sauchiehall Street. It's one of the main shopping thoroughfares in the city: wide, mostly pedestrianised, well-maintained and downhill all the way. We left the porky pensioner trailing in our wake. When we finally came to a stop, about half a mile away, Vicki began whooping before tying herself up in knots of hysterics. I just stood, trying to regain some composure, double-checking my underwear for any involuntary deposits.

"Woo-hoo, now try and tell me that wasn't a total buzz, Ross, my man!"

I wanted to deny it but, in fact, as the shock wore off, I realised how thrilling the whole thing had been; how much I enjoyed the danger, the conspiracy, the chase. Most of all, it made me think that maybe, just maybe, she liked me after all.

"Aye, you're a mad bitch but it was kinda good fun."

She laughed again then, in an instant, her face hardened.

"Who the fuck are you calling a mad bitch?"

I felt my mouth dry, my stomach flip. I couldn't see it happening but I suspect all the colour drained from my face.

"I ..."

She almost collapsed as the laughter spilled out of her again in a torrent.

"Gotcha! I am a mad bitch. It cannot be denied."

I tried to laugh along but something unsettled me about the way she behaved: genuine mania, unstable, a liability. Thing is, you might be tempted to think of her behaviour as being that of a stereotypical, spoiled, little rich bitch. Bored, looking for kicks, rebelling against her parents with her criminality. Maybe. However, her dad being a proper gangster, with a reputation for breaking bits off people he took a dislike to, suggested something else was at play. She'd have to go a long way beyond stealing a couple of pairs of knickers to outrage him. No, I got the feeling it was more like some kind of initiation for me; a test. I didn't realise it right at that moment - perhaps an inkling, but no more - but this was the start of the roller coaster ride she would be taking me on. It wouldn't be long before we were sitting in the front carriage, both hands in the air, doing loop-the-loops with our seatbelts unfastened.

***

The other woman in my life presented me with a different dilemma. Should I even tell my mum I had a job, never mind who the employer happened to be? Explaining how I'd come by a top-of-the-range, hot hatchback stood out as the main barrier to bluffing it. I could park a few streets away, hope she didn't see me using it, but I'd only be delaying the inevitable. At some point I'd get caught. A friend or relative would give the game away in the passing; complementing me on the wheels, asking where I worked now. Then there were the early morning starts, all-day-long absences and late night returns. I lasted until the Wednesday of that first week before she collared me.

I'd dropped Vicki off around eleven and spent an hour blowing away the cobwebs in the Golf: blasting out Biffy Clyro at top volume, singing along until I felt hoarse; racing along back streets careening along the motorway. I parked up in my street but along from my house, not right out front or in the driveway. The key bleeped, locks clunked into place, indicators flashed; done for the night.

Approaching the house, I could see lights on downstairs. This was unusual so late on a weekday. It looked as if my mum might be waiting up for me. I turned my key, stepped into the hall and heard the sounds of tea-making from the kitchen.

"Ma?"

"Aye, do you want a cuppa, son?"

"Eh, aye, ok, thanks."

I hung my jacket in the cupboard, kicked off my shoes, went into the lounge and flopped onto the couch.

She came through carrying two mugs, one of which she put down in front of me.

"Alright, Ross?"

"Aye, fine, Ma. You?"

She sipped her tea, looked at me over the top of her glasses. Inquisition imminent.

"Fine, aye. Where have you been, son? Oh, and where in the hell did you get the fancy motor from?"

Boom! There it was: the big question, no messing, less than thirty seconds after sitting down and we were off.

"I've got a job, Ma."

"A job? Why didn't you say anything?"

"Aye, sorry. I was just going to see how it went this week, not get your hopes up if it didn't work out, you know? I'm doing a bit of driving, well, chauffeuring I suppose you might call it."

She looked over her specs again, folded her arms.

"Chauffeuring? That sounds rather fancy. Who are you chauffeuring for?"

I felt almost aggrieved about this. Where was the *Congratulations, son?* Where was the *That's great news, son?* Her hackles were up; on the offensive; gestures and tone of voice exuding distrust. Then again, I had been working for a gangster for three days and said nothing about it. She probably held the moral high ground here.

"Look, Ma, I don't want you going mad, ok?"

Now the head went to the side a little, arms remained folded, lips pursed, nostrils flared.

"Right, so who are you chauffeuring for?"

"Tommy Stevens' daughter, Vicki."

Her reaction wasn't quite the one I'd expected. Both hands went to her face and she burst into tears. I didn't know what to do, what to say. I sat there, chewing my lip, waiting for her to say something else. She stood and hurried out of the room. I sat still: unsure, perplexed.

71

It took about ten minutes for her to return. Red-eyed but otherwise composed, she sat down again on the couch.

"How did this happen? How did you end up working for Tommy Stevens?"

"He came round last Sunday, said he had a job for me and to meet him at his garage on Monday morning."

"Came round? What, *here*, to the house?" she said, appearing startled.

"Aye. At first I thought he wanted to see you. I minded him being at Dad's funeral and thought you knew him."

She looked as if she might start crying again but held back the flow of tears.

"I do know him, Ross. I know who he is and what he is. And what he is, is bad news. You have to quit. Just phone him up now, tell him you'll bring the car back and that you're sorry but you can't do it."

Her voice quivered as she spoke, laced with emotion. I could tell there was something more to this than finding out I'd taken a job with a hoodlum. Something running much deeper.

"Ma, that's not an option. I like the job, I've been out of work pretty much since I left school. For once, I've got money, a car to drive around in and I can stop running the gauntlet of the Social every week. Anyway, this is Tommy Stevens we're talking about here, some store manager at one of those 'everything for a pound' stores."

"Exactly!" she shouted. "He's a dangerous thug and you need to stay the hell away from him."

I shook my head, sighed.

"Ma, I'm not stupid. I know he's a gangster, dangerous even, but he won't hurt me. I know he won't. Jesus, he just turned up out of the blue, decided to give me a car and trust me to look after his daughter. He came to me. I don't know why he did but I'm not going to look a gift horse like this in the mouth."

She stood up, walked over to the front window, looked through the blinds for a moment before turning back to face me.

"Son, please, this is serious. Tommy Stevens is not a man you want to be working for or owing any favours to. He hurts people. He kills people ..."

She turned back to the street, the hint of a sob being stifled.

I stood, made my way over to her and put my arm around her shoulder.

"Ma, I'll be ok, honest I will. It's just driving his lassie about the place, nothing heavy. He's not asked me to drop packages off or anything dodgy like that. I promise you, the first time that sort of thing happens, I'll walk. It's an easy job for easy money. I mean, I'm still a bit surprised he gave the job to me, but it's a good job, with decent money and a company car. Do *you* have any idea why he would have turned up here to offer me the job?"

She shrugged me off and went back to the couch, took a paper tissue from the box that perched on the coffee table and blew her nose.

"I don't know why, no. I can't force you to stop working for him, Ross, but if you insist on doing this, I don't want to know anything about it. I don't want any of his money. I don't want him or any of his people coming here to the house. Do you understand?"

I nodded.

"Ok."

She got up, took off her specs, rubbed her eyes.

"I'm off to bed now, Ross. I'm shattered and I've got work in the morning."

"Ok, Ma, 'night."

She didn't reply as she left the room.

I sat down again, made the mistake of taking a sip of my stone cold tea. Gross. Something about the way my Ma behaved smelt wrong. I could understand her being upset, but an undercurrent lurked below this visible outrage and distress. I decided not to push it, for now. As I said: on balance, she held the moral high ground.

***

"Tommy?"

"Aye, and whoever this is, I hope you've got a fucking good reason for calling me at one-thirty in the morning."

"It's Anne."

Silence. Tommy felt disorientated, having only just welcomed deep sleep; the mobile almost hadn't woken him. He swung his legs out of bed, walked across the room, into the en-suite, closed the door but left the light off.

"Anne. How are you doing?" he asked, keeping his voice low.

"What are you playing at, Tommy?"

"Sorry?"

"Why have you given my Ross a job driving your girl around?"

Tommy stretched, rolled his shoulders, yawned.

"Because I needed someone to drive her and he needed a job."

"Don't be a smart arse, Tommy. You know fine well what I mean. What the hell are you doing?"

Tommy sighed. Anne had always been highly strung; lovely, but hard work at times.

"I told you back at the Rosebridge that I'd look out for the wee man after what happened. That's what I'm doing."

"And I thought I made it clear when you turned up at Drew's funeral that I didn't want anything more to do with you or the world you live in. Stay away from my boy, do you hear me? Give him until the end of the week, then tell him he's fired and don't come near us again."

Tommy stood up from his seat on the pan, turned round, lifted the lid and began to piss.

"Ok, Anne, whatever you say. He won't thank you for doing this, though. You do know that?"

"He doesn't need to know I had anything to do with it. Bye, Tommy."

Anne hung up.

Tommy finished urinating and went back to bed.

I exhaled after what seemed like a lifetime and padded back to my room, trying not to let my Ma know I'd been eavesdropping. It may well have been accidental eavesdropping but, when you get caught in such situations, the person doing the catching rarely wants to hear the truth. They're even less likely to believe it. And, talking of the truth, I didn't know exactly what had just happened but something told me she no longer held the moral high ground.

12.

The night club throbbed with music and hormones. I stood near the bar, sipping a coke, stone cold sober – a new experience for me in such an establishment. In reality, I had little choice. I was babysitting the most precious thing in Tommy Stevens' life. Transgressing his rules would be suicide. At least, that's how I thought at first. How I thought before becoming intoxicated by something much more powerful than alcohol; something that impaired my judgement and decision-making skills way more than any drug ever could. That's how I thought before I fell under her spell completely.

It was Friday night. I picked Vicki up from her flat. Daddy must have provided this for her, given she didn't appear to have an income of her own. A very nice pad in the West End; no doubt a far cry from the kind of place Tommy grew up in. I didn't get invited up but, as I hadn't ever been allowed into her secret lair so far, I didn't expect to be. I waited in the street outside for Vicki and her entourage to come down.

As the four girls tottered out on implausibly high heels, I got out of the car and opened the back door for the friends, then walked around and let Vicki into the front. Doing my best gentleman and chauffeur impression.

"Why thank you, my good man," she said in a daft, posh voice, as much for the audience as anything else. The audience thought it side-splitting.

Once in her seat, Vicki gave me a strange look. A smile cracked across her face and she turned to her companions.

"Right girls, this is Ross. Ross, this is my flatmate Sian, that's Tegan and that's Kaylie," she said, pointing to each girl in turn.

All three were babes, it had to be said. Two platinum blondes and a jet-black brunette - none of them natural. Trying hard to provoke a reaction from the male of the species; far too much make-up, big hair and wearing clothes that seemed designed to do little more than make a cursory attempt at obscuring their nipples and pubis. All of it screaming of hours spent preening and preparing earlier that evening.

"Hi, Ross!" they sing-songed in unison, like a bunch of primary school kids welcoming their teacher, then burst into a fit of alcohol-fuelled giggles.

I nodded and smiled.

"Hi, girls."

Vicki winked at one of them. I couldn't tell which one she aimed it at, but it was Tegan who piped up.

"You never said he was so cute, Vicki."

Again a flurry of laughter accompanied my embarrassment. I knew what was happening here but, as any man will tell you, it would have been churlish to complain and madness to fight fire with fire when so outnumbered by tipsy women. In any case, my crippling self-consciousness hampered my ability to compete with them on the flirting or piss-taking front. I expected little mercy on the way across town and, in fact, got none whatsoever.

As soon as we got into the club, the four of them ditched me, heading straight for the dancefloor. I perched at the bar, watching, longing, moping. Deja vu all over again; standing near a night club bar, watching Vicki writhe in time to the music amongst a throng of sweaty bodies, knowing I had no chance of hooking up with her. Occasionally, it looked as if I became the butt of some joke or other when one of the girls would look over and they'd all start laughing. Maybe just paranoia on my part but that possibility offered little in the way of comfort.

After three large cokes I'd had my fill of the fizzy

pishwater. My tongue felt furred-up; my stomach carped; my teeth silently pleaded with me to stop washing them all over with acid and sugar. The cost of it riled me too. This introspective whinging meant I didn't even notice the wee lassie who took up a position at my side.

About five-foot-two, blonde (of genetic origin rather than chemical, as far as I could tell), nicely dressed and attractive without using the trying-too-hard bombast of Tegan and Co. She smiled when I caught her eye. A smile I recognised as being straight out of the Ross Fleming book of awkward first dates. I reciprocated. After all, I wrote the bloody thing.

"Hi," she said. Well, shouted more like, on account of the din being generated by DJ Turdgurgler or whatever the hell name the egotistical twat playing the music liked to be known as.

"Hi," I countered. Christ, I was good at this.

An uneasy silence ensued, made worse by my obviously empty glass and her patently just-been-filled one. I couldn't offer to buy her a drink and she didn't seem too keen to recharge my glass at her expense. Something gave, she relented.

"Can I buy you a drink?"

I felt my skin flush. It's funny how conventions pass almost unspoken between generations. It was no big deal. A girl buying a guy a drink. So what? Maybe it was something to do with it being the first one either of us bought the other but something didn't sit right with me - even though I understood the illogical nature of the feeling. And, given the prices, I should have been happy to accept, no questions or qualms. I had the added pressure of what to ask for. Would another coke make me appear square, not manly enough, like I had a problem with drink, like I was driving a gaggle of drunken women about the town? Would my teeth fall out in protest at being subjected to yet another acid bath? Maybe a single beer would be ok? Just a small bottle. That couldn't hurt.

"Eh, aye, thanks. Bottle of Bud, cheers."

American beer: overpriced and over here. Not my first choice in normal social circumstances, but it would have to do.

She turned to try and attract the attention of the bar staff.

Out of the corner of my eye, I sensed movement. In a flash Vicki grabbed me and dragged me out onto the dance floor, into the midst of a rhythmic melee and away from the little blonde. It dawned on me I'd not even managed to ask her name. That Sade song from the eighties, *Smooth Operator*, popped into my head. I wondered if it was possible to be more useless around the opposite sex. It didn't take long for me to confirm that it was possible – if your name happened to be Ross Fleming, that is.

Vicki led me over to where the Witches of Easterhouse were dancing. Draping her arms around my neck, she leant in to my ear.

"Who was that?" she drawled.

I couldn't get my head to stop spinning. My hands had gone to her hips automatically as she put her arms around me. I thought for one awful moment I might faint; make an even bigger arse of myself in front of her than usual. It wasn't only the physical contact, the proximity of her mouth and my skin making me reel. That question. Could she be jealous? Surely not?

"Eh?" I said.

I heard her fine, I just wanted her to come in for a second pass. A dangerous tactic. The stirring in my groin signalled danger. Having her realise she'd invoked tumescence wouldn't do at all – I'd never hear the last of it.

"I said: who's blondie?"

"Don't know, just met her. Didn't get a chance to ask her name," I said.

Despite my best efforts, I rose to the occasion and she knew it. She pulled away, moved closer to the other three and confirmed my worst fears.

A slight lull in the music arrived at the most inopportune moment and, as the cacophony momentarily abated, she screamed, "Ha ha, girls! Turns out wee Ross here is a big hard man after all!"

I knew what she meant; they knew what she meant; the whole fucking club knew what she meant. I wanted to contact the Enterprise and ask Scotty to beam me up. The girls were in hysterics. I slunk off to the bar, trying to disguise the excitement in my trousers. Strangers' mirth and derision followed behind me as I went.

Of course, there was no sign of the wee blonde ... or the beer.

My night was complete.

Only it wasn't.

Not by a long chalk.

At four o'clock in the morning Vicki came across to the bar, leading some drunken, shaven-headed arsehole by the hand. She smiled; the kind of smile I knew could only mean one thing. Trouble. More specifically, trouble for me.

"Right then, Ross, time for you to take me home. This is Dylan."

He reached over, forcing me to shake hands, even though I'd rather have punched the smug bastard's lamps in.

"Alright?" he mumbled in greeting. "Hope that didn't give you a boner, wee man?"

The two of them found this pant-wettingly funny.

I walked off to get my coat from the cloakroom, trying not to look back or show my discomfort, my fury. With all our coats retrieved, we made our way outside. The air hit me like a frying-pan in the face; like returning from a foreign beach holiday where you've spent two weeks in a Mediterranean furnace, and stepping off the plane into what feels like Glasgow's deep freezer. It's even worse in the winter. I shuddered and zipped up my jacket. The shaven-headed wank put his coat around Vicki's shoulders. How very gallant of him.

I refused to say another word to either of them; walking ahead a few paces, keeping out of earshot. I could tell he was itching to continue ripping the piss out of me if I let him. On reaching the car, I got in without waiting to open the door for Vicki as I normally would. They arrived a few seconds later, giggling and grappling.

Once they were both in the back seat, I fired up the engine and drove off.

"Where's he going then?" I asked.

I could see Vicki in the mirror, extricating herself from his tongue.

"He's coming back to mine, where do you think he's going?"

I shook my head, "I don't think Sian's going to be too happy about that."

"It's got fuck all to do with her or with you, so just drive us back to the flat and shut the fuck up, Ross. Right?"

"Aye, you heard the lady, wee man. Just drive us or I'll give you something to fucking whine about," was the wank's unwelcome contribution.

I didn't reply. Bile rose in my throat, my skin prickled, nausea churned. She treated me like dirt but it only seemed to make me want her more. I couldn't stand watching that Neanderthal pawing her. What the fuck was wrong with me?

I tuned out of events in the back seat, turned up the music and made sure I drove as erratically as I could. I took every corner with gusto, braked over-hard and accelerated with ferocity, attempting to throw them about in the back as much as I could. A petty and insignificant revenge but a necessary one as far as I was concerned.

I snapped my attention back to them when they started smoking some weed.

"Vicki, what the fuck? Is that dope?"

"Aye, how? Do you want a wee toke?" she said, passing the roach through the gap between the front seats. I actually admired their ingenuity and determination. Rolling a joint while I'd been impersonating Colin McRae couldn't have been easy.

"No, I bloody don't. I'm driving and your dad would fucking kill me if he found out."

"Oh, for fuck's sake, Ross! Stop going on about my fucking dad will you? He's not going to find out unless you tell him. And you're not going to tell him, are you?"

I let out air in disgust and exasperation.

"No, are you fuck," added Dylan the wank.

This tosser clearly fancied himself as some kind of hard nut; he thought he could intimidate me and make himself appear more masculine to Vicki. I battled the overwhelming urge to call him out on his assertion that he'd give me a doing. I quite fancied my chances, what with him being as pissed as…and me being stone cold. My grip on the steering wheel tightened, knuckles whitening. I really wished somebody had taught me a ninja death grip instead. I'd have used it on that prick in a heartbeat. That's when things took a real turn for the worse.

Blue lights in my mirror.

"Fuck! It's the polis," I hissed.

A panicked Vicki scrambled about the back seat, put down the window and chucked her joint away. I used the buttons on my door to fully open all four windows, trying to clear the distinctive odour from the interior of the car. The sudden cold blast made me shake with a violent shiver. As the police got nearer I closed the windows again. They flashed their headlights to confirm it was our car they were interested in. Now I knew we were deep in the brown stuff. I say *we* were. Of course, the reality was only one person in the car would be wading up to their knees in excrement. Neither Romeo nor Juliet in the rear had anything to worry about. Especially after Vicki leant forward and pushed something into my pocket.

"You need to take this; my dad will kill me if I get charged for possession."

I looked at her, anger scorching through me like a fireball.

"And I'll be fine, will I?"

"Fucking chill out, wee man. You'll be alright. These days, they'll just give you a caution. No biggie," said the wank.

I pressed the brakes harder than I'd intended, pulled into the side of the road, killed the engine.

"Listen, you fucking tit, if I wanted your opinion I'd fucking ask for it. Right?"

He bristled and thought about squaring up, but the police's arrival dampened his ire.

"Can you step out of the car please, sir?" said the huge cop, his fluorescent yellow jacket doing a sterling job of making him even more obvious than his giant frame already managed to.

I did as he requested.

"Do you know why I stopped you tonight, sir?" he asked, adopting that patronising neutral tone their training insisted upon. Calling me *sir* despite being old enough to be my dad.

"No, but I wasn't speeding, I know that much," I replied, trying not to get too defensive too early. After all, thanks to the Queen of Pain, I now held an unknown quantity of an unknown illegal substance. There was no guarantee all she planted on me was hash.

A steady nerve; avoid suspicion or conflict and this would all be over without incident. I thanked fuck for being sober.

"No, sir, you weren't speeding. However, we noticed a defective brake light ..."

Bullshit I screamed inside my head.

"... and then, when we put our lights on, we noticed one of your passengers throwing something out of the window. We have reason to believe that may have been drugs of some sort."

I tried not to look back toward my traitorous mistress but my head shot round in reflex. The other cop, a woman, opened the back door and nodded to her colleague. The airing must have failed to mask all traces of the hash. I felt my pulse quicken, my mouth dry.

"Do you have anything about your person that you shouldn't have, sir? Any substances you'd like to tell me about before I search you?"

I put my hand in my pocket, finding a small plastic bag. I took it out and handed it over, praying it was only a little bit of weed, nothing Class A - that would spell total disaster.

The cop took it, held it up in the light of his torch.

"Thank you, sir. Can you confirm that this is cannabis?"

I nodded and he turned to Vicki and the wank.

"Ok, can you two get out of the car for me please? My colleague will need to search you as well, thank you."

The cops exchanged a few words with each other, asked me if there was any more dope, asked if it was just for my own use, asked if any of us were carrying any weapons, needles or the like, searched us all and the car; found nothing. With all that done, the bloke took me to their car and put me in the back.

He took my details.

"Have you had any dealings with the police before, sir?"

My heart sank.

"Yes."

"So, when I check your details on our computer, we'll have a record of you?"

"Yes."

They certainly would find a record.

Strike three.

Fuck!

13.

The wee dog trotted along beside Tommy, tongue lolling, occasionally jumping up to receive a pat on the muzzle or head. Tommy's scraped knuckles didn't appreciate its sandpaper licking too much but it didn't matter. He'd saved the wee mite from a couple of dickheads intent on giving him a doing. Tommy turned the tables, knocked fuck out of them and decided to take the pooch home.

He decided to call him Dugsleash, in honour of his favourite Scottish football player, Kenny Dalglish. Tommy thought everyone would consider it hilarious. The dug in question was a mongrel, approaching Jack Russell territory but smaller, less robust – the epitome of cheek and fun. They walked together, sun beaming down, not a care in the world. Tommy was sure Paul would love the cheeky wee scamp too.

Tommy walked through the gate-less entrance to his front garden. Dugsleash scurried ahead, scratching at the front door. He tried to get to the wee dog, stop him from incurring the wrath of the much bigger beast inside but he was too late.

Ian Crawford: stepfather, arsehole, violent bully, opened the door in a fit of rage.

"What the fuck is that scratching at my door?"

His door? The bastard only moved in a few months ago. The dog skipped about Crawford's feet, trying to elicit a pat in the same way he had with Tommy on the way there.

"He's called 'Dugsleash'," said Tommy.

The dog was flying through the air toward Tommy before he could react. It hit him in the chest, yelping as it fell to the ground, Tommy knocked onto his arse, winded.

Crawford walked forward and started kicking at the defenceless little dog.

"Dirty little bastard! Keep your shitty arse away from my front door!"

Tommy screamed in protest and threw himself at Crawford, pushing him over onto his side. The dog scampered free, out through the gate-less entrance and away. Gone.

Crawford got up, grabbed Tommy by the hair, dragged him into the downstairs hallway and slammed the door behind him.

When the final blow brought the attack to an end, Tommy lay still for a bit, waiting, making sure his stepfather had definitely left the room before uncurling from his defensive foetal position. The sound of the front door crashing against its frame confirmed his safety. He flexed his fingers, rubbed his arms. As he stood, searing pain circled his ribcage. He dabbed at his nose with an index finger and it came back red. He felt a drip fall onto the front of his t-shirt.

Hobbling, thanks to a dead leg, Tommy went into the bathroom to clean up. Looking in the mirror, he promised himself this would be the last time. The last time that bastard caught him unawares; the last time he touched Tommy ... or Paul. Things were going to change.

With the blood staunched by a bung of toilet paper, Tommy climbed the stairs to the bedroom he shared with his younger brother. Every step sent pain shooting around his body like a pinball, colliding at random with bone, muscle or nerve ending, bells ringing in his ears. Half way up he saw stars, swooned, and thought he might tumble backwards but grabbed the bannister and steadied himself before continuing.

Tommy opened the door, wondering what he might find this time. Anxiety clawed at him; he felt his chest tighten, his heart race.

Paul sat on his bed, knees pulled up to his chest, damp eyes, a bruise rising on his cheek. Tommy hated these moments. The times when Paul realised his big brother couldn't protect him, that no-one could. Fury, resentment, self-pity, self-loathing, guilt, fear; a multitude of emotions vied for space inside Tommy's addled head. Fury won out.

This latest guy turned out to be the worst of a bad bunch their mother had inflicted upon them. In the four years since their real father decided to opt out of his responsibilities, via the front of an underground train, she seemed incapable of attracting anyone other than predators and bullies. Men with little time for children other than as playthings or punchbags. Tommy wasn't sure which was worse: the sexual advances or the violence. This latest arsehole didn't have a particular preference. But, no more. This was where it ended.

Tommy sat down next to Paul and put his arm around his shoulder.

"I'm sorry, Paul."

His sibling looked at him with an expression that conveyed more than any words could. It was all he needed in order to harden his resolve, confirm his intentions.

Ian Crawford, one of the boys; liked a laugh, liked a drink, liked to abuse kids. None of his drinking buddies had the slightest clue about his behaviour behind closed doors – he kept his vile predilections well hidden. They wouldn't be well received if they became common knowledge. As far as they knew, Crawford was a stand-up guy; normal.

The money ran out on the ninth pint, signalling the end of his binge in the pub. He wasn't too put out about it - it wasn't the only alcohol he'd consumed that day. In any case, he had more back in the house.

That snotty, bastard kid with his smelly little mutt looking like a glorified rat, scratching the paintwork off his door, pissing and shitting everywhere. He'd make sure Tommy understood the error of his ways when he got home, reinforce the lesson, leave no doubts.

"Right boys, I'm off. See you all tomorrow."

A round of acknowledgements and goodbyes came from his companions as he drained his glass, headed for the door.

The semi-darkness and warm air of a Scottish summer's evening greeted him. Such benign calm conditions came around so infrequently, they should be savoured. He lit a cigarette and inhaled deeply. Both of the wee shits could wait for a bit. He'd walk home, enjoy the weather ... enjoy the anticipation.

**

Tommy went into the newsagent, picked up the local paper, smiled at the headline.

BODY FOUND IN CANAL IDENTIFIED

Police have revealed the identity of a man whose body was recovered from the Forth and Clyde Canal last week. He's been named as 32 year old Ian Crawford from Ruchill. He was discovered by fishermen last Monday morning. Police say they are not treating the death as suspicious.

It appears that Mr Crawford may have fallen into the canal after a heavy drinking session and drowned. Friends have confirmed that he was not a good swimmer.

The article continued but Tommy had seen all he needed to see. He put the paper back in the rack and walked out of the shop. His companion looked pleased to see him.

"Come on Dugsleash, let's go down the park and see if we can't get you some doggy style action!"

The wee mongrel barked and jumped up before scampering off ahead of him.

14.

If I was annoyed by how Vicki treated me when the cops turned up, I was dismayed at the way she stood by as her dad sacked me. He fired me the day after we got stopped by the police - the day after she made me the fall-guy for *her* law-breaking. As I stood there, receiving my marching orders, I thought she might have told him I'd been arrested or that maybe the police contacted him about insurance details, that sort of thing. I felt betrayed, my loyalty to her thrown back in my face; it didn't seem to me like she'd fought my corner at all. I was wounded by the idea that she couldn't even be bothered to say goodbye, never mind express thanks for all I'd done for her. Then I remembered the call my Ma placed to Tommy the night she found out I was working for him. How she'd insisted he let me down gently. Granted, I only heard one side of the conversation but it seemed as though she'd won the argument and he'd caved.

When I say Tommy sacked me, in reality, Ralph Bonner did the honours. He took the Golf's keys back from me, gave me three hundred in cash and sent me on my way. He enjoyed every second. It brought home to me how little I really meant to Tommy that he didn't bother to do the dirty deed himself. I walked home through drizzling rain; thinking, fuming, plotting.

My anger threatened to boil over but, somehow, I found the sense not to head straight for a showdown with my interfering mother. In her mind she was looking out for me and, if I could be honest with myself, I should never have gotten mixed up with a gangster. She was right, I was wrong, but I couldn't just lie down and take it. If you'd been out of work and flat broke for as long as I'd been, then had a gig as good as this one ripped from your grasp, I don't think you'd just lie down and take it either. I spent the journey towards home deluding myself about personal safety, the morality of my employer, the long-term prospects this job offered.

Deep down, I knew where my real issues lay: with Vicki Stevens. Gorgeous, temptress, conceited, headcase, diva, bully. And yet I was giddy with lust, desperate not to be separated from her. This was what really bothered me about losing the job. The money, the car, all the other stuff meant nothing compared to spending time with her. She'd done nothing to encourage my desire; done nothing to deserve my loyal servitude, but reason appeared to shuffle out of my brain for a wee break whenever thoughts of her bubbled up. My obsession was as bad as any junkie's: focussing on my next fix, ignoring the potential damage and the negative effect it had on me.

My next fix came later that day. I realised Ralph had forgotten to take back the mobile phone Tommy had given me. I found a bus stop; got out of the rain. I took out the phone. There were four numbers to choose from.

I decided to make the call.

It was the only way to deal with the situation, to try and make things right.

One call.

That's all it would take.

I punched in the number.

The phone rang.

"Vicki?"

"Ross? Is that you?"

"Aye."

"How are you doing? I'm sorry about what happened last night. You ok?"

Genuine concern, or going through the motions? I couldn't tell. As usual, I didn't much care one way or the other. We were talking, that's all that mattered.

"Aye, well, there you go, I'm alright I suppose. Well, I

thought I was until this morning."

"Why, what happened this morning?"

Motions or emotions? I still wasn't sure.

"Your old man gave me the bullet."

There was a pause at the other end of the line.

"Eh?" she said, this time definitely not faking it.

"What? You didn't know?"

"No, I bloody well didn't know! Did he give you a reason?"

"Not really; he wasn't there. When I came to pick you up this morning, Ralph was waiting for me. He took the car keys back, gave me some money and told me I wasn't needed any more. That was it."

I suspected Vicki's displeasure over my sacking owed more to her ego and control-freak tendencies than anxiety about my welfare. It wasn't the fact I got punted, it was the fact she didn't get to do the actual punting, at a time of her choosing, that mattered.

"What an arsehole! He never said a word to me about sacking you. When I asked why you weren't driving me today, he said he'd given you a couple of days off; that I shouldn't expect a seven-day-a-week service. What was that all about for fuck's sake?"

She went quiet again. I liked to hear her rant; the passion, the fire in her. I did a bit more stoking.

"Ah, well, I don't suppose there's much I can do about it, Vicki. Thing is, I've got this phone and I'd like to get it back to your dad, but I'm a bit embarrassed to phone him to arrange returning it."

Of course, I deliberately omitted the Ralph option; tried to get the response I wanted. It worked.

"Where are you now?"

"I'm at a bus stop. I was walking home but stopped to call you."

"Walking home? But it's pissing down out there. Did Ralph not offer you a lift?"

I snorted, "Eh, funnily enough, no, he didn't."

"Right, I'll meet you in The Fort, at the coffee place we usually go to. In about an hour. Ok?"

Oh, it certainly was, but it wouldn't do to seem too keen. I needed to keep pressing the buttons.

"I don't know, Vicki. Your dad might not be too chuffed, seeing as how he sacked me. Maybe he thinks I'm some kind of pot-head waster after last night and doesn't want me anywhere near you?"

"Fuck my dad! How would he know about last night? Did you tell him?"

"No, what makes you think I would do something as dumb as that?" I replied.

"Well, neither did I, so it can't have anything to do with the dope."

"Ok."

"Right, that's it, Ross. I'm meeting you. An hour. See you then."

"Ok, see you then."

She hung up.

Job done.

I almost shat myself when I walked into the coffee shop and there, at her favoured table, sat Vicki - with Tommy at her side. I hoped they hadn't looked my way, tried to avoid eye contact. Too late: she'd seen me, waved me over. Tommy sat, stony faced, sipping coffee and reading a newspaper.

"Hi," she said as I approached.

My heart thudded in my chest, like I'd run the whole way there rather than taken the bus. I felt sick, weak-kneed, sweaty. I tried to swallow but failed, due to a total absence of moisture. The best I could muster was a nod.

"You getting a coffee, Ross?" she asked.

Tommy only glanced towards me, giving nothing away.

"Aye," I managed to squeak. "Do you want anything else?"

"No, I'm fine. Do you want anything else, Dad?"

He let the paper fall into his lap, put the coffee on the table and looked straight at me with those reptilian eyes.

"To get back to my house and the horse-racing on the telly, actually, now that you ask."

My fear ratcheted up by several notches. It was like that moment he appeared on the doorstep out of the blue all over again, with my sweat glands and heart rate responding with exuberance to his mannerisms and the tone of his voice.

She shot him a sneer before turning to me, "On you go, Ross. Go and get yourself a coffee."

I decided coffee might not be the best option, so I bought a bottle of juice. It would lubricate my parched oesophagus without having to wait for it to cool or run the risk of causing third-degree burns to my mouth. I could also forego worries about my shaking hands leading to embarrassing spillages.

I took a couple of swigs from the bottle as I walked back to the table. I pulled out a chair and sat down opposite father and daughter.

"Dad, do you want to tell him? Or shall I?"

Tommy looked across at me with that unwavering cold stare.

"You want the job back, son?"

"Eh, aye. If that's ok, like?" I stammered.

"Well, turns out, Vicki likes you and pleaded your case, so I decided to give you another chance."

I wondered about getting brave; letting him know I knew all about my Ma's intervention - but decided against it in the end. I liked the current arrangement of my body parts, the way they all connected to each other; I didn't think it wise to encourage him to consider separating them.

"Thanks," was all I went with in the end.

He got up, folded the paper under his arm and finished his drink. He leaned over and pecked Vicki on the cheek.

"See you later, Vicki."

She nodded.

"I need a wee word, son," he said as he started to walk away.

I followed him without question, doing a tremendous impression of a faithful wee dog. About fifty yards away from Vicki he stopped, took the keys to the Golf out of a pocket and put them in my hand.

"Just one thing, son. Probably best not to tell your Ma you're working for me. She doesn't approve. Ok?"

I felt relief wash over me.

"Aye, that's fine, Tommy. I'll not say anything to her."

Other than to tell her to stay the fuck out of my business I thought.

"Right, I'm away. See you later."

"Aye, see you later, Tommy."

Back at the table Vicki thumbed her phone, barely registering my re-appearance.

"Thanks," I said, after a minute or so of silence.

"Eh?" she said, not even raising her head from the screen of her phone.

"For getting me the job back. Thanks."

She looked up, popped the phone into her bag, "Yeah, whatever. Look, I need a lift. I'm going shopping with Tegan but we need to pick her up at her flat. Did my dad give you the car keys back?"

"Aye."

"Good, let's go then."

Normal service resumed.

Back in the saddle.

I couldn't have been happier.

We stopped at some traffic lights and I happened to glance back at her. To be completely honest, I spent more time looking at her in the rear-view than I spent looking ahead at the road. It was a minor miracle I'd not run into the back of anyone else because of it. This time we were stationary, so the risk of accidental collision was greatly reduced. She seemed to be scribbling in a little note book. I couldn't be certain what it was. I thought it might have been a diary but it didn't really look like one. She saw me looking and stopped.

"What?"

I looked away, guilt streaking across my face, shook my head, shrugged.

"Nothing."

I heard her mutter something indistinct but definitely containing the phrase 'nosey bastard'. It took every ounce of my rather limited self-control not to look again. I lasted for at least seven seconds, glanced back.

"Fuck's sake, Ross. You want a fucking picture?"

I didn't have time to dwell on my mortification as the car behind hooted his horn in frustration at my lack of response to the green light. I think it may only have been one nanosecond, maybe two, since it changed - despite my distraction. I put the car into gear, gave the prick the finger and roared away. He gave chase for a couple of streets but lost out to the superior speed of the Golf and the eventual divergence of our respective routes.

"Take a right here," she said, out of the blue. I was confused. Taking a right wouldn't lead us toward her friend Tegan's place as far as the sat nav was concerned.

"I thought we were going to Tegan's? Sat nav says to go straight on here."

"We are, but I need to check something first. Take a right here, will you," she replied, exasperation clear in her tone.

I did as she asked. Actually, there wasn't a lot of asking involved. It was much more like an order than a polite request.

"Stop somewhere here, where you can get a space."

Again, I complied with her wishes. We were lucky: a car pulled out in front of us and I slid straight into the space they left.

She didn't speak, seemed to be watching the street up ahead. A normal Glasgow street with normal cars and normal punters going about their normal business, the odd normal bus rumbling by, a cyclist braving the normal wind and rain. Tenements stretching up for a few stories atop small shops and commercial premises. A dentist's surgery, a bookies, a couple of pubs (one boarded up and fire damaged), a newsagent, grocer, an estate agent. A couple of more exotic imports: a Polish food shop and a shop selling cloth for making saris and other traditional eastern garments. All normal. I couldn't see anything out of the ordinary. After a few minutes she moved us on, back on track to Tegan's house.

The rest of the day passed without incident.

When the shift finished I went home and kept quiet about my return to Tommy's employ, parking the car outside Vicki's flat and taking the bus home from there. I also avoided any unnecessary confrontation with my Ma. I had the upper hand if she found out and started hurling accusations. She'd know she had no right to interfere like she had.

I kept my powder dry.

I might need it later.

15.

"We're going round to see my Uncle Paul," said Vicki.

"Right," I replied.

I knew Tommy had a brother, given the sign on the garage and the advice to avoid phoning him unless I really had no other options, but I hadn't met him yet.

"There's something you need to know first."

"What?"

"He's disabled."

"Oh, right," I replied, a bit unsure why I needed to be pre-warned about something like that.

"What I mean is: he's stuck in a chair, paralysed from the neck down. He had a bad accident when he was younger; broke his neck."

"Shit, that's terrible."

"Yeah, it is. Thing is, he's not always glad to see visitors. Especially new folk, so just chill, don't react if he gets a bit aggressive. Ok?"

"Aye, fine," I replied.

Her family seemed determined to make my interactions with them as fraught as possible and Paul would prove to be no exception.

The house was big. Not quite a mansion, but not far off. A large, adapted vehicle sat out front on a butter-smooth asphalt driveway. Shallow ramps extended up to the front door, presumably to help improve wheelchair access. Wide, flat paths criss-crossed the large garden where well-tended raised beds blazed with colour. The whole place looked immaculate; cared for.

Vicki rang the bell. A stunning Asian woman dressed in white opened the door, beaming a perfect toothpaste-advert smile.

"Hello, Miss Vicki, nice of you to drop by and see your uncle!" she gushed.

"Hi, Zhang Li, this is Ross," said Vicki, walking past the nurse and on into the entrance lobby.

"Hello, Ross. Nice to meet you," said the beautiful vision in white, extending her hand for me to shake.

"Hi, nice to meet you too," I said. The hand shake lingered as I found myself entranced by her perfect skin, glossy black hair and chocolate-brown eyes.

"Want to put your tongue away, Ross, and come and meet my Uncle Paul, now?" snapped Vicki.

I felt my face glow, saw Zhang Li look away as we broke our grip. Was that another wee sign of Vicki's jealousy when another woman showed any interest in me, or I showed signs of being interested in them? More likely, she didn't like having female competition in the looks department at any point – whether I was there or not. Felt threatened and insecure, despite all that front; the comment as much about making the nurse feel awkward as it was an attempt to embarrass me. It worked. On both counts.

I moved past Zhang Li, shrugging a sort of apology and followed Vicki through the house to a large open-plan living room at the rear.

The room looked like it had been designed to combine ease of access with sensory overload. Pictures covered almost every wall, plants and flowers adorned tables and shelves. A massive TV hung on one wall, cartoons crashing about on the screen, muted and unwatched. Paul Stevens sat in front of two massive patio doors in what looked more like a state-of-the-art military vehicle than a wheelchair. Canisters of oxygen fed a clear piece of tubing, which ran around his face and under his nose. A blanket covered his lower half. A wispy, scruffy-looking growth of facial hair accompanied straggly, greying locks which framed a gaunt face. His striking blue eyes narrowed as I approached.

"Hiya, Uncle Paul," chirped Vicki.

"Who the fuck's this?" was the caustic reply, his voice laboured; rasping.

"This is Ross. He's driving me about now."

I nodded and Paul bared his teeth like a pissed-off dog, "Well, he can get himself to fuck."

Vicki looked at me and shook her head.

"Come on, Uncle Paul, that's not very friendly now, is it? He's just giving me a lift so I could come and see you for a wee while."

She leaned over, kissed him on the forehead, then sat down opposite him on a leather sofa - the only significant piece of furniture in the room. I shuffled, looking at my feet, uncomfortable again, unsure whether I should leave or go over and sit next to her.

Paul looked at me, licking his lips in a slow, rather unsettling manner. Not so much lascivious as predatory.

"So, Ross the toss, you got a surname or what?"

I so wanted to get out of there. This obnoxious bastard was enjoying making me squirm, goading me, trying to get a rise. The chair, his condition, they didn't excuse him being a total prick to me. Vicki gave me another look that said 'grin and bear it', for her sake. So I did. A mistake; I should have gone with my instincts.

"It's Fleming," I told him.

Fire flashed in those intense, sharp eyes. He swallowed several times in rapid succession, his prominent Adam's apple bobbing up and down like that fairground game where you use a hammer to try to ring a bell.

"Fleming? Ross Fleming ... you're not Drew Fleming's laddie, are you?"

"Aye, that's right."

The grimace returned.

"Your dad was a wanker, a woman-beating low-life. Got what was coming to him. I can't believe Tommy gave you a job. Then again, he always did have a soft spot for the hopeless cases, the waifs and the strays, the poor little orphans. Isn't that right, Victoria?"

She glared back at her uncle. I'd had enough.

"Right, I'm away back to wait in the car, Vicki. Your uncle doesn't want me here and I don't have to listen to him slagging my dad off – even if he is in a chair."

I began to walk away and Paul started clucking, "Like father, like son; a little yellow bastard who can't take the heat. Aye, go on, fuck off out of my sight. I never asked you here in the first place, you wee dick."

I stopped, thought about replying; thought about punching the twat. Of course, I didn't follow through on that thought. I would never stoop so low as to batter a guy in a wheelchair. Probably. I kept walking and he kept up the chicken impersonations, right up until the door closed behind me.

Out in the car, I fumed, trying to take stock of what Paul Stevens said to me. He claimed my dad got what was coming to him; called him a low-life, a wife-beater and a coward. If Tommy knew my dad, it stood to reason Paul would have too. What I found odd, though, was Tommy attending the funeral of someone his brother held in such contempt. I couldn't help wondering if either of the brothers had some kind of involvement with his death... But, if my dad and the Stevens used to be enemies of some kind back in the day, why would Tommy give me a job? That wouldn't make sense. Confusion fogged up my brain.

My mum told me my dad died in a car crash. What if that wasn't true? What if she lied to me about how he died in order to protect me from the truth? I knew so little about my dad and my mum never seemed keen on helping me fill in the blanks; evasive and vague whenever I raised the subject. We'd moved out of the city and had little to do with any relatives on his side of the family since the funeral. It never bothered me much. I got used to it, the way things were. Maybe I needed to push her harder to get some answers?

The barbed comment directed towards Vicki intrigued me as well. It was such a weird thing to say in front of a stranger. Was he implying she was an orphan, or a stray? The fog only thickened.

Paul Stevens came across as an angry, bitter man; railing against the injustice of his situation; venting his anger on others – yours truly included. All his bile and spite towards my dad would likely turn out to be nothing more than a wind-up. After I'd had time to reflect on things I realised if I was stuck in that chair, I'd likely behave in the very same way.

I waited thirty minutes for Vicki to reappear. I had to give her top marks for patience and determination. She must still see something in the man which made it worth her while enduring the abuse. Then again, maybe he'd put on a little show of strength; reminding me of who he was, what family he belonged to – despite the chair and the disabilities. Maybe, as soon as I was out of the room, he switched to sweetness-and-light mode?

"What was that all about?" I asked as she got into the back of the car.

"Oh, that's normal. I warned you about it before we went in. He's got a lot of anger issues to work through. He's a nice guy when you get to know him."

"Right," I said. "Not sure I want to."

"Anyway, let's go. I want to hit the shops now, do some serious damage to Daddy's plastic!"

I drove off, Paul Stevens' cryptic comments bouncing about in my head as we went.

16.

"I can't take any more, Cath. I've had enough!"

Margaret's despair had been creeping up on her for months. Tonight it tapped her on the shoulder and shouted 'boo!' when she turned around. She felt trapped; hemmed in by other people's judgement of her life choices. Disappointed in herself, disgusted by the dark thoughts taking over her mind. Terrified about what might happen. A black pit yawned in front of her, beckoning.

"I know things have been difficult, Mags, but you've got the bairn to think about. She needs you."

The tears stopped at last, the hysteria subsided. At least for now. A calm descended on Margaret McLean.

"The bairn will be fine with him. I can't trust myself any more. I need to go, to get away. Before ..."

Cath so wanted to help her sister banish the madness gripping her mind, causing her to think about harming the wee one. The first couple of times she'd heard Mags snap it seemed normal; the kind of thing any young mother might do when fatigue and exasperation took hold. Nothing serious. But it got so it was constant. The bairn never seemed to do anything other than irritate Mags and provoke angry outbursts, just by behaving as all babies do. The smack and the shake signalled something else; something less understandable, less forgiveable. Cath couldn't keep quiet or ignore it.

The unavoidable confrontation about it hurt both of them. Cath tried to bully Mags into going to the doctor or telling the health visitor. She tried using emotional blackmail and idle threats. Nothing worked. Mags refused to get help from the authorities, convinced it would mean Vicki being taken into care. She knew if that happened,

Jimmy's wrath would be fearsome. The sisters parted on bad terms but tonight, three days later, Mags called round with the wee one in tow and went into meltdown in Cath's front room.

"Jimmy can't look after her, Mags. He's never in. I mean, you know the kinds of things he gets up to."

"He loves her, but."

It was true: Jimmy did love Vicki. Cath couldn't deny it, but his lifestyle was all wrong.

"I know he loves her, Mags, but when did he last change a nappy? Make up a bottle? Give her a bath?"

"You could take her," said Mags, her voice barely audible.

Cath looked at the broken shell that used to be her sister, sitting there in front of her: eyes dull and lifeless; hair lank and greasy; no make-up; wearing a curious mismatch of clothing, none of which seemed clean or ironed. She looked like she'd lost weight. This, from a young woman who once took such pride in her appearance. Cath knew if she didn't help Mags break free something terrible might happen to her precious niece. Her precious sister, for that matter.

"Where will you go?" asked Cath.

"I'm not sure. I thought about Newcastle. I know a couple of people there; I could maybe get a job in a hotel or something. It wouldn't be forever. Just some time to let me get my head sorted out."

Cath looked down at the floor then; across at the baby sleeping soundly in the pushchair. She took Mag's hands in hers.

"Ok, I'll help Jimmy look after her. You need to get well, see a doctor, get some medicine. Right?"

"Right," whispered Mags. "Thanks, Cath."

The two women embraced.

"I love you, Mags. All I want is for you to get better," said Cath.

Mags could only manage to nod, as tears flowed for

both of them.

After a minute or so Mags stood, wiped her eyes, gathered up her bag and coat and went over to the pushchair. She bent down, stroked the little girl's head, kissed her forehead and rubbed her tiny hand.

"I'm so sorry, Vicki. I really am. Mummy will come back for you soon and everything will be alright again. I promise."

Mags turned to her sister again and they hugged one more time.

"Look after her for me, Cath. Tell Jimmy I'm sorry."

Cath let her sister out and stood in the open doorway, watching her walk away into the night. It would be the last time she ever saw her.

17.

Random bouts of riding round town, with Vicki insisting on taking odd detours and unplanned stops, became commonplace. At least, I considered it random to begin with. The notebook or diary or whatever it was made more appearances. I tried to avoid conflict by becoming more subtle in my furtive and lustful observations. In a different life I might have thought we were both spying on someone. Little did I know how close to the truth that would turn out to be.

On a Tuesday morning, after we'd stopped for no apparent reason outside a butcher's shop, Vicki scribbled something in her little book, thinking her actions to be surreptitious. As she did so, I looked across the street. Ralph Bonner came out of a bookies carrying a hold-all, looked left and right, then climbed into the gleaming black Audi I'd seen so many weeks before in front of Tommy and Paul's wee garage. I couldn't make out if there were any passengers through the dark-tinted windows. He put on his indicator, signalling his intent to move away, and Vicki's response was instant.

"Let's go."

"Where?"

"Eh, just drive for a bit. I'm going to give Sian a buzz, see if she wants to go for lunch."

"Ok."

I pulled away, suspecting we might be following Ralph, rather than killing time waiting for Sian to confirm her social calendar had opened up. Unlike Vicki, Sian's daddy didn't provide for her every whim and she needed to work to pay her share of the rent; a beauty therapist or something like that, I think she said. When Vicki insisted we took the same three turns as Ralph, then stop when he did, I knew for a fact we were following her dad's right-hand man. It might also mean we were following her dad as well, if he was ensconced behind darkened glass in the rear of his limo. She began to enter notes into her book again. I decided to brazen it out.

"Why are we following Ralph about the town, Vicki?"

She stopped writing, looked at me with eyes wide, her expression a mix of guilty discomfort and anger.

"What the fuck are you on about?" was her rather aggressive reply.

"I'm just wondering why you've been getting me to follow Ralph Bonner about the place."

She slammed the book down and leant through the gap between the two front seats.

"What's your fucking problem, Ross? All you're supposed to do is drive me about, take me where I tell you I want to go. What's with the constant spying on me and all these stupid fucking questions about what I'm up to?"

I wasn't going to rise to the insults; I'd keep calm and keep going with my line of questioning.

"Alright, Vicki, but I'm just interested in why you've had me tailing Ralph this morning. I saw him come out of the bookies back there and as soon as he left, so did we. You made me follow every turn he took and now we've stopped again while he went into that bookies," I said, pointing across the street. "Then there are the notes you keep writing in that wee book. I'm curious, that's all."

"What do you think my name is? Jason fucking Bourne? Why would I be spying on Ralph or my dad? And I've told you before, what I write in my book is none of your bloody business, you nosey bastard."

Again, I chose calm over conflict.

"Ok, I just wanted to mention it. Thing is, if *I* noticed we were following him, there's a pretty good chance *he's* noticed *us* following him too. Like you said, it's not like we're a pair of highly trained CIA operatives. Just thought

I'd point out that if you are tailing the guy, for whatever reason, he'll most likely have spotted us."

I could almost hear the thought processes inside her head clunking and clanking away. For the first time, I saw a pink tinge of embarrassment creep across her face.

"You're fucking cracked, Ross. I'm not following ..."

At that moment, Ralph Bonner rapped on the window of the car and we both jumped out of our skin. I pushed the button and the window slid into the door.

"Alright?" was his verbose opening as he leant down to address us.

"Aye, no' bad. You?" I replied.

He gave me the evil eye and turned his attention to my passenger, "Alright, Vicki?"

"Yeah, fine."

"You don't need me for anything, then?" asked the big man.

"No, why?"

"Just wondered why you've been driving around behind me this morning, that's all. Thought maybe you needed me for something, so I just came over to check, like. I was going to do it the last time you stopped but your dad called and asked me to come here. When I saw you stopped again I thought you must be needing me for something, right enough."

I'd never seen Vicki so unsure of herself; so obviously uncomfortable. He was laying it on thick, letting her squirm.

"No, we weren't following you for anything, Ralph. We were just cruising, waiting for Sian to let me know if she was coming for lunch. It's just a coincidence, I never even noticed you," she lied. I wasn't convinced. I didn't think Ralph would be either.

"Ok, no worries. I'll be on my way then. See you later, Vicki."

She nodded and I replied, "Aye, see you later, big man."

He looked at me as if I were something he regretted stepping in, and walked away, the same hold-all in his hand as before.

I pushed the button to close the window.

After a few moments of silence, I noticed Ralph drawing away from the front of the second bookies.

"You want me to follow him?" I said, but couldn't keep a straight face as I did so.

"Piss off, Ross!" she said. "Take me over to Sian's beauty parlour so we can pick her up. She's just texted and said she can make lunch."

I pulled away and drove across the city to Sian's work. All the way there Vicki sat with her elbow propped on the door, her hand against her face as she looked out the window. She didn't speak to me much for the rest of that day.

18.

Tommy Stevens stood at the bar, his nearly-full pint of lager nothing more than a prop. He rarely drank to excess any more, preferring the safety and certainty of a clear head. It would be all too easy to be caught unawares by an enemy while inebriated. Anyway, he'd had his fill of getting bladdered, making an arse of himself and spewing up; that kind of carry-on was a younger man's game. Distracted, he fidgeted with a beer mat, turning it end over end against the counter top.

Somebody with very poor musical taste managed to find the jukebox and put on a couple of horrid pop songs he didn't recognise. Some wailing banshee with vocals he thought would be better suited to terrorising dogs than entertaining humans – almost bad enough to tempt him into abandoning his sobriety.

He only frequented this shitty bar because of her. To be near her, to talk to her. The place lacked any other redeeming features. Every time he came in, with each conversation he engaged her in, he edged closer to asking her out. Tonight would be the night he finally found the bottle to follow up one of their flirty chats with an offer of a proper date.

Cath Donaghy arrived for her shift around seven, delighted to see Tommy Stevens already in his usual position at the bar; waiting for her. As presumptuous as it may have sounded, she knew it to be the case. According to the other girls who worked the bar and to Dougie, the owner, he never stopped for a drink if she wasn't on shift - or just about to arrive. They teased her something rotten about the obvious crush he had on her. Very tall; a bit on the thin side, not that good-looking in any classical sense.

His allure may not have been conventional but he had something else: charisma, character, a presence. He could hold a decent conversation and, although she found him humorous, he never acted like a village idiot or a mouthy show-off in order to get laughs. He'd been coming in for weeks and each time she saw him her heart quickened. She wished he would pluck up the courage to ask her out.

"Hi, Tommy," she chirped in her usual, friendly manner. He took her gaze. She loved those grey eyes - so unusual.

"Hi, Cath, how's you tonight?"

"Good, thanks, Tommy. And you?"

"Aye, not too bad, thanks. All the better for seeing you, mind."

She blushed and waved her hand towards him. She felt the butterfly flutter he so easily induced in her.

Some other punter ordered a beer. She grabbed a glass and pulled down on the tap. Tommy watched her pour, his eyes following the contours of her figure. She was in knockout shape. He loved the way she tied her hair up, the subtle make-up, the slight kink in the bridge of her nose, her dark-brown eyes, the way she giggled. It dawned on him at that moment, in that shitty bar, as he watched her pour someone else a drink, that he loved everything about her. He had fallen in love with her.

Tommy's life was a long way from what might pass as 'normal' in the real world. He'd survived a shooting and a follow-up attempt to finish him off; taken his revenge on The Boss and most of his gang; and, one of his main rivals came to a sticky end (ahem) after an ill-judged extra-marital affair. His brother almost died, but surviving left Paul reliant on a nurse and a host of technology. All of this turmoil established him as a serious player in the Glasgow underworld, and with that status came headaches, responsibilities and danger. It caused him to shy away from serious romance; the promise of a family, any semblance of normality; but something about this girl made it impossible to resist her.

"Cath?"

"Aye?"

"Can I ask you something?"

"Aye, what?"

"I was wondering."

"Uh, huh?"

Cath felt like screaming at him to 'spit it out'.

"Do you fancy going out for a bite to eat some time?"

"With you?" she said, winking.

He felt heat prickle across his skin, "Eh, aye, with me. What do you think?"

"Oh, ok then, why not. You got somewhere in mind?"

He so didn't have somewhere in mind. It was all his brain could cope with to organise his thoughts into a coherent question. There was no space left for things like which particular restaurant they might go to or what kind of food they might eat. He'd spent no time contemplating what he might do in the event of an affirmative answer.

"Eh, not really. I thought maybe Italian? Do you like Italian?" he said.

Italian: a safe option that rolled off his tongue automatically without any need for deep consideration or planning.

"Italian sounds good."

Tommy arrived at the little family restaurant early. He always arrived early for appointments - business and pleasure alike. He'd been shown to his seat, ordered a nice glass of red. The place had been recommended to him by his cousin Steve who knew the owner and arranged for VIP treatment.

He sat there waiting, discomfited, unsettled. These days folks did what he said, turned up when he told them to. He'd gotten used to it. This was taking him well out of his comfort zone. It felt like being back at school again, with all the awkwardness and self-doubt of his teenage years returning like a bad dream. The stupid thing was, he'd become good with women in the intervening period: confident, charming, successful in persuading them to think sleeping with him might be an enjoyable experience. Most women. Cath Donaghy seemed to be bucking that trend.

When she eventually did arrive, her tardiness and the time spent waiting dissolved into irrelevance. When the waiter took her coat off to hang it up, it revealed a figure-hugging red dress and matching high heels. She looked stunning. It made the look she chose for work appear dowdy in comparison. Her hair, always tied up in the bar, fell below her shoulders in a sweep of dark brown gorgeousness. He'd never experienced the sort of overwhelming wave of emotion that crashed over him at that moment.

They spent an enjoyable couple of hours getting to know each other. He learnt a lot about her. Her hopes, fears, ambitions. Even the revelation that Cath had been forced to assume the legal guardianship of her sister's wee girl, after both parents vanished without a trace, didn't put him off. He usually avoided complications like girls with some other guy's sprog in tow. But Cath was the one. He thought she might be while he watched her pour drinks in the bar. He became more convinced after the meal. The deal was sealed beyond all doubt by the time they collapsed in a heap on his living room floor, having failed to make it to the bedroom such was the lust that overcame them as soon as his front door clicked shut behind them.

Six months later they were married and he became proud stepfather to a beautiful little girl called Victoria.

19.

My Ma was crying. I felt like joining in. Three months in jail, suspended for a year. I escaped a much worse fate thanks to nothing more than the luck of the draw in terms of which Sheriff heard my case. Last proceeding of the day for an old duffer who appeared desperate to get home for a good spanking from his dominatrix or rent-boy, such was his haste in dealing with me. My Ma's tears were as much from embarrassment and disappointment, as from relief. Mine, if I'd let them flow, would have been exclusively related to relief.

Vicki and Tommy didn't attend court with me. Just as well really, as my Ma wouldn't have been best pleased to see either of them. Vicki was under the impression I'd only received a caution for possession and I did nothing to dispel that notion. I pleaded guilty, which meant she didn't need to give evidence as a witness and neither did that knob-end she hooked up with that night. I probably got a few Brownie points from the crumbly old Sheriff for my 'honesty' as well.

I hadn't told Tommy about the court case either. I thought it best not to. If he found out, I expected to be on the receiving end of a far worse punishment than anything the court could dole out. I didn't imagine him rating the idea of a hash-head driving his precious daughter about all that highly. On the other hand, I could have dropped Vicki in the shit; grassed her up for dropping *me* in the shit - but that didn't appeal as an option either. I'd have burned all my bridges at once if I'd done that, she'd be furious and Tommy would no doubt think me a disloyal Judas. Not a winning combination. No: I sucked it up, kept it to myself. When I needed to present my documents to the police it required a bit of subterfuge. I used the same bullshit excuse the cops did when they stopped me. I told Tommy they'd invented a faulty brake light so they could stop me and, even though it was fine, they still insisted I needed to bring my documents in at a later date. I made out I was the victim of harassment for being a young guy in a flash car. He gave me the insurance cover note without any proper interrogation, told me that sort of thing was an occupational hazard, brushed it off.

So, I got away with it.

Just.

It was only when we got outside, finished thanking the lawyer and began walking towards the car that my Ma laid into me.

"What the hell is wrong with you, Ross?"

"Look, Ma, we've been over this! I said I'm sorry. Fuck's sake."

She glared at me, unimpressed by the defiance and the language. We took a taxi home in total silence, unable to find the right things to say. There wasn't really anything *to* say.

That night I found myself back in a club, propping up the bar with my orange-and-lemonade. I tried all manner of soft drinks in order to attempt to convince myself that abstinence wasn't so bad after all. It didn't work. I'd been waiting around for two hours, desperate for the assorted members of Vicki's coven to pull and fuck off, or give the order to go home.

For some reason, that night Vicki hit the drink much harder than usual. She was wasted before they even got into the club but continued to down shots with the others until, in a near state of collapse, her pals brought her over and asked me to take her home.

In order to get her to the car, I had to put her arm around my shoulder, while I slipped my arm around her waist. The feel of her body up against mine was one of the highlights of my life up to that point. This time, I didn't worry about any stirrings in my trouser department as she was too drunk to notice or care.

I poured her into the back seat and, as I leaned across to put her seatbelt on her, she grabbed my face with both hands and kissed me. Not a peck: a full-on tongue sandwich. I almost fainted in ecstasy. After a few seconds she drew away, leering, eyes rolling in her head.

"Ha-ha! You've been hoping I'd do that for months, wee Rossie-poo, haven't you? Well, happy birthday, little driver boy!" she slurred.

I stood back, stunned and deflated. My absurd hopes of the kiss marking the beginnings of a seduction had been smashed to pieces. I closed her door and got into the driver's seat, my heart thumping, my stomach doing cartwheels, my groin throbbing. Adrenalin surged through me; I couldn't concentrate, couldn't work out what to do next.

"Ross, Rossie, I don't want to go home. Take me somewhere to get a coffee, there's a good little driver boy."

I didn't answer, I just started the car and began to drive.

She lolled to the side, righted herself, then repeated the exercise twice more. On the third slip she went over to the same side as the door and passed out.

It was about one-thirty in the morning. I couldn't think where I might get us both a coffee. Then I remembered about the twenty-four hour services on the motorway. There was a set of those not too far out of the city.

Vicki had taken a bit of rousing once we got to the service area but, after a quick trip to the bathroom to eject some of the excess alcohol, she began to recover.

We'd been sitting opposite each other in the franchised coffee outlet for about half an hour or maybe an hour; I'd not taken too much notice of the time when we arrived. Vicki downed two coffees in quick succession, becoming more coherent in action and voice with each passing minute. She'd started the third but slowed the pace of consumption by a considerable margin and nodded off again.

I sat looking at the beautiful wreckage in front of me and couldn't help but feel violated. Ridiculous? Maybe. The thing was, although I'd dared to dream of the moment she and I would kiss, I never imagined for one moment that if it did happen, it would be part of some sneering piss take. She'd never treated me well but this seemed harsher, with an edge of cruelty to it. For the first time, I began to doubt whether I even liked her, never mind loved her.

"Ross, I'm sorry about all this," she said as she woke.

I sensed my anger and hurt receding. I never imagined myself being such a soft touch but I must have developed that trait when I wasn't looking.

"Aye, it's alright. You got hammered. It's fine."

"No, it's not fine, Ross. You've been lovely to me from the day you started and I've been a total bitch to you."

"Aye, that's true," I joked.

"Hey, you weren't supposed to agree with me!" she said, folding her arms and pouting, pretending her feelings had been hurt.

I toyed with the empty polystyrene cup in my hand, not sure where to look. She'd gone from harpy to goddess in an instant.

"I shouldn't drink so much; I can't handle it."

"You were going for it, right enough. I don't usually see you drinking like that. How come you were trying to get so blasted?" I asked.

She looked away, toward the windows behind me and the darkness outside, her eyes welling up. I began to sense something I'd never seen in her before: vulnerability.

"There are some things about me you don't know, Ross. I'm not who you think I am. More than that: I'm not who *I* thought I was."

"Very mysterious, very deep," I said, winking.

"I'm serious. Things have been building up for months and tonight I just couldn't take any more. I needed to get wasted. Try to forget."

I returned to twirling the cup. I couldn't pin down exactly why this conversation made me uncomfortable. Something in her tone, the hurt in her eyes; at odds with her usual bravado and über-bitch persona. A loud sniff brought my focus back.

"I need to tell you something. Something you can't tell anyone else, ok?"

I shrugged, "Ok."

"I mean it, Ross. This is between me and you, right? You can't breathe a word to anybody else."

I began to sense the hairs on my neck rising. This was huge. She was going to confide in me. It represented a sea-change in our relationship, indicated a level of trust reserved for people you really care about, that you know won't let you down. My heart began to race.

"Ok, Vicki, I get it. I'll keep it between us; promise."

Our secret.

"About six months ago, I went round to my mum and dad's. I didn't tell them I was coming, a kind of spur of the moment thing, you know. Anyway, I walked up the path and I could hear them fighting. They never fight so I was a bit surprised and a bit scared. I went round the back of the house and was about to go in through the kitchen when I overheard what they were fighting about."

She took a sip of the coffee in front of her and pulled a face, "Urgh, this is stone cold. Can you get me another please, Ross?"

I got up and went over to fetch her a fresh brew. I ordered a tea for myself. At the prices they charged in this place, I found myself running seriously short of readies. If she asked for another after this she'd need to get her purse out. As I stood waiting for the order I heard her phone go off. I knew it was hers as she'd customised the ringtone to play a Kanye West track. I thought it was utter pish; she thought it was total class. That's music for you.

I made my way back toward the table, put the drink down in front of her and sat back in my seat, ready to hear the rest of her story.

"No, he's back. ... I need to go ... Yes ... Aye, see you later ... Yep ... Bye."

"Who was that?" I asked.

She turned her stare into a sharp implement, then softened in an instant.

"Oh, it was Sian. She was worried about me, just checking I was ok."

"That was nice of her, looking out for her mate."

"Aye, she's a great pal. The best."

We settled into a silence. I didn't think it appropriate for me to prompt her on with her story. She appeared to have lost momentum. After a few sips of her coffee, she continued.

"Anyway, as I was saying, my mum and dad never fight. I could hear her shouting at him. They were arguing about me. I thought at first it would be about him spoiling me and giving me too much money and all that bollocks. The usual shite."

"I take it, it wasn't?" I said.

"I wish it had been. No, they were fighting about my real mum and dad."

Her face crumpled, she struggled to compose herself. I didn't get it.

"What do you mean, your *real* mum and dad?"

"Turns out, I'm adopted - but it's worse than that. I think Tommy killed my real dad and kept my real mum away from me."

Once those words left her mouth, she lost control of her emotions: sobbing, tears falling freely. I got up and went round to her side of the table, putting my arm around her shoulder. She snuggled in and used my jacket as a makeshift towel.

"That can't be true, Vicki. You must have misheard them or got the wrong end of the stick," I said, still trying to get my own brain round this revelation.

She shifted up and shrugged my arm off her.

"No, it's true. Otherwise, why would Cath have left him the next day?"

"Cath?"

"My mum, well, the woman I thought was my mum."

This was nuts.

"What did Tommy say? Did you ask him about it?"

"Of course not! What was I supposed to say – hey, pretend dad, did you kill my real dad and stop my real mum from coming to see me? I did ask him where Cath had gone but he won't talk about it. He says it's between them and it's nobody else's business."

"Have you spoken to Cath?"

"No, she's vanished. Anyway, we never got on and now I know why."

We sat in silence again for a few moments. I tried to get my head around how this must have been affecting Vicki's behaviour. It explained so much of the tension and anger. It also cleared up Paul Stevens' snarky comment about waifs and strays.

Fatigue swept over me; the lateness of the hour, the pumping hormones and the emotional stress taking their toll.

"Vicki, let's go home. We can talk more about this tomorrow if you want. You need to get some rest, get a decent kip," I suggested.

"Yeah, I suppose. We can't stay here all night. Let's go."

We stood and shuffled out from the booth. She leaned over and kissed me on the cheek.

"Thanks for listening, Ross. And sorry about earlier," she whispered.

I couldn't find my voice to reply and instead combined a shrug, nod and smile.

Our secret.

20.

"It's the only way, Sian."

"I don't like it, Vicki. It doesn't seem right."

Vicki got up from the settee, walked across to the TV and switched it off.

"I know, I feel bad, but I have to make this happen. That bastard cannot get away with what he's done."

"Yeah, I get that, but is this really the only way?"

Vicki crossed her arms and gave Sian her special laser stare.

"Ok, ok, I get it. Let's get on with it then," said Sian, realising she would not be changing Vicki's mind. It was ever thus.

Sian McDonald had known Vicki for years. They met in dancing class and had been inseparable ever since. The problem for Sian was the one-sided nature of their relationship. Vicki called the shots, Sian did her bidding. Over and over again Sian mentally castigated herself for being such a doormat, such a weakling, but Vicki held a spell over her. She should be saying no to this stupid, reckless plan but, as usual, she didn't say no. She never said no to Vicki. The truth, the hidden truth she'd never managed to get Vicki to see, was that Sian loved her. Sian ached for Vicki; longed for her to notice her feelings as much more than friendship - but she couldn't jeopardise it all by being the one to blink first. There would be no way back if Vicki rejected her advances. She'd rather have what she had now than risk never seeing her again. Even if what she had now was little more than unrequited subjugation.

Sian wasn't sure if she was a lesbian or not. Apart from her powerful attraction to Vicki, she'd not noticed other women piquing her interest sexually. Then again, she never seemed to find lads all that attractive either. It was Vicki she wanted. Just Vicki. If that made her a lesbian, then so be it. She didn't mind what label got applied, the end result was all that mattered.

The buzzer rang.

"Ok, that's him. Let's go," said Vicki.

It's funny how things can happen right under your nose without you noticing them. Blatantly obvious things. How it escaped me up until that point remains a mystery to me. Sian's not that common a name; hardly exotic either but, even so, a little unusual. My mate Big Mac told me his sister Sian was an old pal of Vicki's back in the club when I first saw her. And yet, after months of driving Vicki around and hearing Sian's name mentioned numerous times, as well as keeping her company on multiple occasions, I failed to make the connection. Until this moment.

Vicki came out of the door to her flat, Sian followed behind.

"Can you give Sian a lift to her dance class, Ross?"

Light bulb.

"Dance class? Sian, have you got a brother called Gerry?" I asked.

"Aye, why, do you know him?" she replied, looking and sounding rather suspicious.

"Yeah. Not seen him for a wee while, mind you but we used to go clubbing together."

"Oh, right. I don't remember him mentioning you," she said, getting into the back of the car.

I took my seat behind the wheel.

"Aye, well, how's he doing anyway?"

"Fine. Dodging away, as far as I know. We're not that close, to be honest. We lead pretty separate lives. Where did you meet?"

"A mutual friend organised a football match, we got picked to play together and that was it."

"Right," she said, clearly losing interest and becoming entranced by her mobile phone.

"Isn't that weird, though? Spending so much time together and not realising," I said, chuckling.

"Yeah, I suppose," was the end of the conversation. She and Vicki began to discuss something to do with the dance class. I zoned out. Not a topic I could muster any enthusiasm for or contribute to in any meaningful way. It was good to see my winning ways with women hadn't left me.

After dropping Sian off, Vicki asked me to take her to the coffee place. She wanted to chat. I began to think, to hope, that she regarded me as much more than her driver. It transpired that she did. But, right then, I could never have guessed what that would turn out to mean.

We got a couple of coffees and took up station at the usual table. Vicki seemed tense; pensive, stirring her drink far more than was required to dissolve the single sugar she'd added to it.

"I went to see Uncle Paul, although, he's not actually my uncle at all as it turns out. Anyway, I asked him about my real mum and dad and what happened to them," said Vicki.

"And?"

"It's not good, Ross. Paul's a bitter man: he hates everyone - but it means he loves delivering bad news. He told me Tommy killed my dad, way back, when I was only a tiny baby. My real dad was part of a rival gang who were planning to kill Tommy but Tommy got in first."

"Holy shit! That's heavy as fuck. Are you going to go to the cops?"

"No point. Paul says there's no way I could ever prove it. They were very careful getting rid of the body. It's too long ago and there are no witnesses, if you catch my drift."

I didn't know what to say to her. This was about as fucked up as it could be. I expected tears, or some kind of emotional outburst, but it never came. She remained calm;

a hard edge to her. They may not have been related after all but there was more than a touch of Tommy about her.

"What are you going to do?" I asked.

She looked down into her cup, holding it with both hands, gently swivelling it around.

"Ross, I need to ask you for help."

I felt the familiar adrenaline rush she invoked in me.

"Ok, what do you want me to do?"

She looked up, those gorgeous dark eyes drawing me in.

"You know how you've asked me about my little book and why we were following Ralph around that time?"

"Aye."

"Well, I've got a confession to make. I've been planning my revenge against Tommy. Ralph is his bagman; collects money from the bookies. I'm going to rob him."

"Are you fucking mad?" I exclaimed, realising when she said '*I'm*', she had no real intention of doing the deed herself.

"Probably, but I have to try and get back at that murdering bastard."

"That's fair enough: if it was my dad he'd killed, I'd want to get my own back too - but what good will robbing him do? He's loaded, he'll probably not be that bothered."

She looked a bit pissed off at me, like I was stating the bleeding obvious.

"I know that! I'm not a fucking idiot, Ross. This is the first part of a plan to disrupt his life, annoy him, wait for a chance to cause his downfall."

I took a drink and drained my cup.

"Ok, sorry, I didn't mean I thought you were stupid. What about Ralph? He's a fucking gorilla! How the hell are you going to persuade him to part with the money?"

She finished her drink and stood up.

"That's where you come in. We can't keep talking about this in public. Let's go to my flat, I've got something to show you."

This should have been the best invitation of my life, a chance to see the inner sanctum, my mistress' lair. In any other context it might have implied the promise of carnal delights; a delicious *double-entendre*. Instead, I felt queasy, ill at ease. My chances of enjoying what she wanted to show me seemed remote.

"Fucking hell, Vicki, it's a gun!"

I stepped back from her, reeling from the enormity of this.

"Yes, I know. It's how we'll get Ralph to give us the money."

Her calm demeanour, her matter of fact delivery was almost as scary as the hunk of metal she held out toward me.

"When you say *'we'*, Vicki, I take it you mean *me*?" I asked, trying not to sound too much like a whiny schoolgirl. I failed.

"Jesus Christ, Ross! I thought you cared about me; I thought you'd be happy to help me," she shouted, before stuffing the gun back into the cloth bag it came from and sitting down heavily on the couch.

"I do want to help you, Vicki. It's just a shock, you know? I'm not a gangster. I've never even seen a real gun, never mind used one before. I'm sorry."

I sat down next to her as she began to cry. I put my arm around her and she moved in close to me.

"I don't want him to get away with this, Ross," she said, sobs interrupting the flow of her speech. "I need to get him back for this. I want to find my mum and try to get my real life back."

"I know, but this?"

She looked at me with damp eyes, and kissed me. Tenderly, not like the frantic piss-take of the other night. I responded. Our mouths locked together for what seemed like minutes. When we broke free I could hardly see, my head whirling like a fairground ride gone out of control. She stood and took me by the hand, led me to her bedroom door. I struggled to breathe properly. She kissed me again, this time starting to remove my clothes. I tried to reciprocate but my fingers felt like a bunch of bananas. I couldn't work buttons or zips, never mind have any chance of dealing with a bra clasp. She pushed me onto her bed and finished the job of undressing herself. I was overwhelmed by the vision of naked perfection in front of me and, when our skin made contact, I realised this was real: we were going to make love.

Afterwards, I lay on top of the bedclothes: sweaty, panting, exhilarated. Vicki sat up, swinging her legs over the side of the bed.

"Ross, I really need you to help me. Will you help me?" she said glancing over her shoulder.

I propped myself up on my elbows, "Yes. Ok. I'll help you."

She smiled, turned back and began to kiss me again.

21.

I don't know why I thought my mum might tell me something new about my dad's death. She'd stuck to her party line for so many years. But today was the big day. The day we'd rob Tommy Stevens. I felt infused with vengeance on behalf of both dead fathers. I was more convinced than ever that Tommy must have been responsible for my dad's death as well as Vicki's. Him, or Paul, or maybe both of them. On this day of all days, I wanted to get to the truth; to know my mission was righteous.

We were having breakfast when I asked her. I opted for blunt.

"Did Tommy or Paul Stevens kill my dad?"

She dropped her toast onto her plate and adopted an expression I'd rarely seen since the halcyon days of my early childhood.

"What the hell kind of question is that?"

"I want to know the truth, Mum. Did either of them have anything to do with Dad's death?"

"No, they didn't!" she said, the pitch and volume of her voice rising. "I've told you before, it was an accident. He crashed his car into a tree. So, what's put this stupid idea into your head?"

I couldn't get her to crack. She would stay true to her story. I knew I was wasting my time.

"Nothing. It's just that you reacted so badly to me working for Tommy and you never talk about Dad. It's been bugging me."

Her face softened, "Ross, son, I don't talk about your dad because he and I were on the verge of splitting up when the accident happened. He wasn't a good man but

I've never felt it would be right for me to trash your memories of him. I don't need you to hate him as well. He never treated you badly. It was the only thing he ever did right by me, though."

She stood up, scraped her toast into the food recycling bin and poured the remains of her tea down the sink.

"There's nothing more I want to say about this, Ross. Ok? I'm going to work. I'll see you later, son."

I let her go.

I'd thought of someone else who could tell me what really happened to my dad. A person who'd be only too happy to help.

I heard the bell chime far off inside the house. A cold breeze nipped around my ears and nose as I waited. I blew into my hands and stepped from foot to foot, trying to stay warm.

"Hello. Can I help you?" asked Zhang Li. Her smile as bright and friendly as I remembered it. She really was a stunning looking woman.

"Hi, yes, it's Ross. Vicki's friend? I came round here with her the other day when she came to visit her uncle."

"Oh, yes, I remember you now. How are you?"

"Yeah, I'm good, thanks. I was wondering if I could have a wee word with Mr Stevens, if he's around, like?"

She looked a little confused, "Is Miss Victoria with you?"

I shook my head, "No, I've come by myself. Mr Stevens said he knew my dad. He died when I was little and I don't know much about him. I hoped Paul, eh, Mr Stevens, might be able to tell me some things about him I didn't already know."

I tried to inject a dash of puppy-dog into my delivery; to play on her empathy or sympathy. She was a nurse after all. It was her job to help people.

"Oh, I'm sorry to hear about your father. I'm sure that'll be ok. Come in and I'll go and see if Mr Stevens is awake and will speak to you."

"Thanks a lot," I said, stepping into the hallway and the welcome hit of warm air from the central heating.

Zhang Li walked off up the hallway toward the large room where I'd had my previous altercation with the younger Stevens brother. She returned a couple of minutes later.

"Ok, Mr Stevens says he will talk to you. He's in the living room."

"Thanks."

"And good luck, I hope he can help you find out good things about your father," she said, as she sashayed away in the opposite direction.

I smiled and waved in appreciation, "Ta."

I knocked on the door and entered without waiting for permission. This didn't please Paul Stevens all that much.

"Aye, come in then, you little prick," he snarled, as I walked around to face him.

"Hello, Paul."

"Paul? Paul? Where the fuck do you get off calling me Paul? It's Mr Stevens to you, got it?"

"Aye, whatever you say, *Paul*."

I'd decided I would only get the truth from this prick if I riled him. Otherwise, he'd be in control and could feed me whatever line of bullshit he thought would have the biggest effect on me. He took the bait.

"You listen to me, you little cocksucker. I might be stuck in this fucking chair and have to eat through a straw, but I can still arrange for you to be force-fed your own bollocks. Do you understand?"

"Yeah, yeah. Listen, last time I was here, you said my dad got what was coming to him. What did you mean?"

He laughed. A sinister, gloating laugh.

"Oh, dear, what's the matter, son? Hit a raw nerve did I? Miss your daddy, do you? Oh, poor wee Rossie-wossie."

"Look, you spastic dickhead, just tell me what you know."

I wasn't proud of my lapse into playground taunting. It felt wrong using that kind of insult to gain the leverage I required, but "needs must" and all that.

The fury in his face was something to behold. I wondered if I might have found the way to get his severed spinal cord to heal itself and allow him to get up and beat the living shit out of me. I knew a little bit about Paul Stevens' reputation before the accident. I was glad it didn't actually happen. The fury passed, transformed into a sneer. The look of a man who held all the aces. My bravado began to crack and splinter.

"You want to know what happened, do you? Ok, as you asked so nicely, wank-stain, I'll tell you. Your dad was a faggot, a loser who liked to beat women. Your mum liked to play away from home. Not a good combination. She hooked up with our Tommy, rode him like a mechanical bull, so she did."

I could feel my own anger building. This was what I feared: that he'd come up with some outlandish bullshit to try to get to me. I shook my head.

"Oh, don't shake your head, son. She certainly liked the boaby, your mammy. She *really* liked Tommy's boaby. Anyway, one day they're riding like a couple of rabbits on Viagra when your arsehole faither turns up with a gun. Your mammy wants to blow Tommy while your daddy wants to blow him away!"

The laugh returned. I fought with my emotions but I knew I was giving too much away; encouraging him.

"However, and this is the best bit, it really is. I mean, you'll never guess what happened next. Can you guess, Ross? Can you, son?"

"Fuck off, Paul. This is all a load of shite. You're just trying to wind me up, you prick."

"Really, dick-face? Does that mean you don't want to guess? Well, if you can't guess, I'll just have to tell you what happened. Your dad bursts in; finds your mammy bouncing up and down on Tommy's pink pogo stick. He puts the gun against Tommy's head and he's going to pull the trigger but, before he can do that, guess what happened? Go on, you want to guess now, Ross, don't you?"

A cold shiver swept over me. I knew what he was going to say next. I wanted to stop him speaking but I was stuck to the floor, glued in place. My brain appeared to be wired up wrongly, refusing to send accurate signals regarding speech and any manner of other bodily functions.

"That's right: your mammy took Tommy's other stick and lamped your daddy with it. Cracked his skull like an egg, so she did. And that was that: goodnight sweet Drew, it was nice knowing you. Actually, it wasn't, but there you go. Your whore of a mammy killed your wanker of a daddy. Did the world a favour as far as I'm concerned."

The anger that raged through me at that moment was the greatest I'd ever known. A combination of hatred for this vile, gloating paraplegic, revelling in my discomfort and horror at the realisation that he could never have made such a thing up on the spot. My mum killed my dad and lied to me about it, inventing a bullshit accident to appease me. It explained the job: Stevens owed her, so he helped me out. It explained her nervousness about him, her animosity.

I felt the room shrinking around me, constricting my thoughts and breathing. An eerie silence swallowed all other sounds apart from Paul Stevens' taunting laugh, which reverberated inside my head. The fury spilled over. My hands went to his scrawny neck, I began to squeeze. His eyes burned back at me, defiant.

"That's it, son," he croaked. "Kill me, kill me, motherfucker. I can't wait to get out of this fucking chair. I'll say hello to your daddy when I get to hell!"

I squeezed harder, trying to shut him up. His eyes bulged, still defiant, still taunting me.

He didn't resist.

He wanted this.

135

He welcomed it.

My brain came rushing back to rescue us both. I let go, staggering back and falling onto my backside on the living room floor.

He coughed and spluttered, "You hopeless little fuck! Just like your useless fucking faither: a pathetic coward. Finish the job, kill me you little bastard. Come on!"

The shouting attracted Zhang Li. She burst into the room, fear and confusion in her eyes.

"Mr Stevens, what's going on? Are you ok?" she said, rushing toward him.

"I'm fine, get this useless piece of shit out of here," he growled, his voice hoarse, cracked.

The nurse fired me a look as I got back to my feet.

"It's ok, I'm going," I said.

Outside, in the car, I sat gripping the steering wheel. Tears tumbled down my face. I couldn't control them. Everything I thought I knew about my family lay in tatters. A smouldering pile of ash and debris. If I was motivated before to help Vicki get her pay back, my own fuelled-up desire for vengeance would make helping her even easier.

I didn't know what I would do about my mum, but she could wait. First up, we'd make a start on sorting out Tommy 'The Stickman' Stevens.

22.

So, now you know how I came to find myself standing in the street, digging a bullet out of Ralph Bonner's skull.

The idea to intercept Ralph and relieve him of a substantial pile of Tommy's illegal earnings went horribly wrong. We used the notes Vicki compiled while I drove her around, selecting a quiet backstreet in which to ambush the big man; one that didn't appear to be covered by any CCTV as far as we could tell. Vicki went to a fancy dress shop and bought me a zombie mask which seemed appropriate because if Tommy found out I was behind it, I was already dead. She also gave me the pistol.

I had mixed feelings about the weapon. I didn't know how to shoot a gun. I mean, where would I have learned such a skill? I may have nicked a bike and a few bits and bobs from shops. I even helped beat a guy to a pulp once. But, I didn't run about with the Ecossa Nostra when I was growing up. I only agreed to carry the gun in order to deter Ralph from exploiting his significant physical advantage over me. Unfortunately, Ralph's loyalty and self-belief were far greater than I thought they might be. If I hadn't shot him, he'd have killed me. I knew this without any doubt. The look in his eyes, the threats and the hunting knife he pulled on me made it quite clear. It also turned out the mask didn't stop him recognising my voice.

Him or me.

In case you're wondering, it was a lucky shot. Not as far as Ralph was concerned, clearly, but, for my part, it represented something of a miracle. One shot: face gone, man down, no knife embedded in my intestines.

I'm running towards the car, which I'd left two streets away. I take off the mask and put it in my pocket. The bag of money doesn't weigh much, even if it does hold a hefty sum within it, so it's not hindering my escape. As I enter the main street I slow to walking pace, letting my breathing settle. I don't want to draw any unnecessary attention to myself. I also pull up the hood on my plain sweatshirt. Just another punter: bland clothing, face obscured, nothing to mark me out from the crowd.

As I turn the corner onto the street where I left the car, I stop. The Golf isn't parked where I left it. I think I can hear the sound of breaking glass all around me. I look around, trying to make sense of the situation. I wonder if I've taken a wrong turn when I came out of the side street, but I haven't. This is the right street - but the car has vanished. I walk towards the spot where I stepped out of it earlier that evening, checking my pockets for the keys. My brain begins to separate sentient thought from blind panic. I left the keys in the ignition. I also left Vicki sitting in the passenger seat. She wanted to listen to some music while she waited on me.

Where the fuck could she have gone? She can't drive, so somebody else would need to have driven the car away.

But, why? Why the fuck would she disappear, at this moment of all moments?

Did she arrange this? Is there something going on here that I don't know about? A set up? Paranoia surges through me.

Has she been kidnapped?

Tommy's words from months ago, about not leaving her alone to bump into certain types of people, leap into my head. I feel sick. If she has been snatched, what am I going to do about it now? I take out my mobile, try to call her. It goes straight to voicemail. In an emergency I'm supposed to call Tommy or Ralph but, for obvious reasons, that option is no longer open to me. I decide this isn't one of those times I could justify calling Paul Stevens either. In any case, I don't think he'd be too keen to hear from me.

I keep walking, racking my brains, trying to dredge up some kind of idea I can act upon to help solve this problem. I should be more vigilant, more aware of the potential danger I'm in, but my mind is not concerning itself with the real world around me. I seem to have teleported from the world I used to live in into some kind of mad new world. A world I need to get out of as soon as I can.

The enormity of everything that's happened today hits me in the face like a shovel. I found out that my mum murdered my dad; I nearly strangled a disabled man to death; I robbed a gangster; I joined my Ma in the murderer's club; and, I misplaced my hot-hatch company car with my super-hot, unstable girlfriend still sitting in it.

I don't notice the van drawing up alongside me. I don't notice the guy get out or his rapid approach behind me. I do notice the scratch of the needle but darkness engulfs me before I can react in any way.

My vision is blurred, my tongue thick and heavy, over-filling my arid mouth. I ache all over; a dull listlessness weighing down on me like I've been forced to carry a bag of coal on my back. I want to reach for my eyes to rub them but my arms won't move from their position down by my sides. Tied. As are my legs.

I can make out a few shapes. Something looms in close to me.

"Good morning, Ross. I trust you slept well?"

Even through the murk I recognise the voice. I can't answer him yet but my vision begins to clear.

"I think he might be awake, Vicki. What do you think?"

A waft of her perfume drifts into my nostrils as she answers, "I think so, Dad, aye."

Confusion grips me. Her voice sounds ethereal, disembodied. Why would she be here? Wherever 'here' is. I try to re-arrange muddled thoughts into some kind of sensible order. Urge my mind to get up to speed with getting me up to speed. Tommy Stevens helps me along the way.

"In case you're wondering what's going on, Ross, you're recovering from a wee sedative I like to give potential troublemakers in order to pacify them. You'll be a wee bit groggy for a while but I'm sure we can increase your alertness."

I hear movement and see a figure approach from my left. They press something against my skin and I jolt in my seat, the shock stabbing into my cloudy consciousness. Pain screams through me, trying to awaken every one of my stuporous synapses. My alertness increases, as predicted.

"That's better now, isn't it?" he says.

Not necessarily, I think.

"Where am I, Tommy?"

"You're in a wee facility of mine. The exact location's not important."

The room is Spartan: unfurnished, walls undecorated and unadorned. The lighting subdued; provided by a few strip lights. The floor is a slab of unpainted, rough-cast concrete. Tommy steps in front of me, arms crossed. He's wearing a white boiler suit. I don't like the look of it; something clinical, sinister, about that kind of get-up.

"I have to say I'm very disappointed in you, Ross. I gave you a job. I let you drive around in a nice car. I trusted you to look after my girl. I reckon that was pretty big of me, even if I say so myself. What do you think?"

I look down at the floor, fear rising through me, creeping along every nerve and sinew. I feel like a bath being slowly filled. Appropriate, given how much hot water I've found myself in.

"I don't know what to say, Tommy. I'm sorry."

He snorts, looks to his left, then back to me.

"I bet you are. Now you've been caught. Vicki told me all about your plan: about how you tied her up, left her in the car and went off to rob Ralph. Well, rob me, as it happens. It's just as well Sian managed to contact me and let me know where she was. "

"What?" I say.

The fear begins to drown me. What bullshit is this? Why would Vicki have done this, betrayed me, fed me to the lion? I look around, but I can't see her. She must be hiding back in the shadows somewhere. Too embarrassed to look me in the eye. How could I have been so fucking stupid?

"We found Ralph by the way. Fuck me, son, you really did a number on him. I was quite impressed, in a way. I would never have had you down as a killer. Oh, and just in case you're wondering, you don't need to worry about the police. I much prefer to keep these things in-house."

I can't form a coherent train of thought, certainly can't find a suitable riposte.

"Why, son? Why would you get so fucking greedy? If you'd kept your nose clean, I'd have seen you right. You could have worked for me for years, enjoyed the perks."

"I..."

"Actually, the money's not that big a deal in the scheme of things. Killing Ralph? That was pretty fucking extreme, but he was a soldier. He knew the risks when he signed up. Doesn't mean I would have let you off with those things. I wouldn't have, to be honest, but that stuff is about money; it's about business. This is a tough game, people let you down. Shit happens."

I notice he's not using his stick as he takes a couple of paces left.

"Aye, it's fair to say I wasn't too chuffed about those things, son. But they're not what's really got me riled. What I can't forgive, what I won't forgive, is messing with my wee lassie and my brother. That's nothing to do with money or business: that's personal, Ross."

My brain finally starts to function with more lucidity. Scenarios, possibilities and options race through my mind like hot needles.

"So, before we finish this thing off, I'm interested to know - why, son? Why would you think all of that was a good idea?"

His demeanour is cold, calculating. Totally calm. For a man who's talking about a heightened state of anger, he's not showing it much. There's a slight edge to his voice but not a lot more.

"I've got a few questions of my own, Tommy. Like, why did you help my Ma kill my Da? And, how exactly did you murder Vicki's real faither?"

He looks at me with a mix of surprise and fury.

"You cheeky little fuck! How dare you talk back to me like that? I plucked your scrawny little arse off the dole queue and gave you a fucking good job. I paid you good money, I treated you well, and this is what you do to show your gratitude?"

There's no wondering about how angry he is now as he moves in close. Right into my face. I can smell sour breath and aftershave.

"I am so going to enjoy this."

He steps back.

"Vicki, it's time, darling."

From out of the shadows, Vicki steps forward, also wearing a white boiler suit. She's holding a gun.

"Vicki, what's going on?" I ask, panic threatening to consume me.

She steps forward, stands in front of me.

"I'm sorry, Ross. It's just how it's got to be. You should never have got involved with me."

I see the gun, I'm looking down the barrel for a split second but I can't look, I'm too scared. I don't want to die. I close my eyes and tense.

The shot rings out.

I wait for the pain but it doesn't come.

I wonder if this is what dying is like; painless; instant; like nothing happened.

I hear a sniff and open my eyes.

I can't decide if I'm in heaven or hell.

Vicki is kneeling over Tommy. He's lying on the floor, a crimson stain spreading across his boiler suit. The gun is still smoking.

"I know what you did, Tommy. I know you killed my dad and I know you've kept me apart from my real mum. Just so you and Cath could play happy families."

"Vicki, I didn't know he was your dad at the time," says Tommy, his breath laboured. He's struggling, grunting in pain between most words. He's on his way out.

"Bullshit! Paul told me about how you felt guilty, how you thought you could make it up to me for killing him. He says it's always been your weakness. What were his words? Oh, aye. *You've got a thing for stray dogs*," she says. It's clear this phrase has really angered her, such is the venom on display when she repeats it.

"Paul said that? What? That's not true. I only found out who your dad was after I married your mum."

"She's not my fucking mum!"

"No, she's your auntie. Your mum asked Cath to watch over you because she couldn't cope. She had that post-natal depression thing."

"I don't believe you. You're a liar. A murdering, bastard liar!"

"Vicki, please, I'm sorry. You don't need to do this. It's all true."

For the first time since he was a little kid, Tommy resorts to pleading. It's not mercy he's after, he doesn't need clemency. This day was always going to come - he knew that - but he never thought his end would be by Vicki's hand. The thing he needs is her forgiveness, to have Vicki believe he only tried to help her. Otherwise, it was all a waste.

"Too late for 'sorry', Tommy. You made my whole life a lie. You kept all of this from me, just so you could pretend to be my dad. Well, fuck you. You didn't have that right."

He goes to speak again, but he's done. I hear his last breath hissing and gurgling out of him. I can't talk. I wouldn't know what to say even if I could.

Vicki looks at me. A couple of tears drip down her cheeks and she gives a weak smile. She walks over to me, unties the ropes binding my hands and feet. I stand up, go to hug her but she steps back.

"No, Ross. I'm so sorry about all of this," she says, "but it's the only way."

Something in her voice unnerves me. I feel weak, disorientated by the drugs and standing up too quickly. I see the gun come up again.

This time, after the report, there is pain.

I'm going down into an abyss.

The pain has gone.

So have I.

23.

"It's done, let's go."

Sian looked at Vicki, reached out and squeezed her knee.

"You ok, honey?"

Vicki nodded and patted Sian's hand, smiling. A smile laced with regret and resignation. Sian started the car and pulled away.

"Where to now?" Sian asked.

"The flat. I need to get a few things."

Vicki looked out of the window, watching other people continue with their lives as normal. Her life had never been normal but now, as far as she could see, it looked like an even more crazy fucked-up mess.

She wished she hadn't needed to involve Ross. He never asked for any of it. Wrong place, wrong time. The thing was, her options got squeezed down to a single point. Did she let Tommy Stevens go on being her surrogate and continue taking his twisted charity, or did she make a stand for her parents and the dozens of others whose lives he'd wrecked over the years?

Vicki realised it would be better to avoid such disingenuous, worthy bullshit. This had nothing to do with the fate of others. She knew what it really came down to: she wouldn't allow herself to be manipulated. Nobody else got to control her life – not even Tommy Stevens. Killing him should have made her feel better, vindicated, but it didn't. Tommy lied. The biggest lie imaginable. But he'd also been such a big part of her life; the only dad she ever knew. He loved her - she knew that to be irrefutable - and, until that fateful moment, standing outside the kitchen and hearing Cath berate him for what he'd done, she'd loved *him* too.

Ross provided a means to an end. A nice guy, but the world wouldn't rock on its axis at his passing. For the first time, she thought of his mum. A brief pang of guilt whispered in the back of her head.

They arrived at the flat. She would be fine. These conflicted feelings would pass. They always did. She had things to do.

The suitcase on the bed filled up with all the light, summery outfits she could muster. Vicki had friends in Madrid. She'd go there and, catch some rays, let the dust settle, then make an effort to find her mother. Her real mother.

She couldn't decide what to do about Cath. Tommy left no room for wriggling. A dangerous, unpredictable thug. With him, she needed to be decisive. In any case, he'd killed her dad and prevented her mum from coming back to her. He deserved it. Cath, on the other hand, merely colluded. She may have been bullied or threatened by Tommy. Maybe Vicki's mum really did have some kind of breakdown and asked her sister, Cath, to look after her baby. Assuming that's who Cath really was, of course. It was hard to trust anything about the people she once knew as family any more.

Vicki wondered why Cath left so suddenly. What could have caused her to do that after so many years? It even occurred to her that maybe she didn't leave of her own accord.

Now was not the time to decide how to deal with Cath. She'd use the time in the sun to figure something out. A plan of action.

"I need a lift to the airport, Sian. Can you take me?"

Sian felt her nerves start to prickle. Why was Vicki fleeing the country? That wasn't part of the plan she'd discussed with her. As far as she knew, Vicki was going to get Ross to rob Tommy in order to goad him into taking action but, before he could hurt Ross too badly, Vicki would get the police to arrest Tommy. Vicki had assured Sian that Ross was fine with this and agreed to help her because he reckoned Tommy was involved with killing his dad as well. Why this sudden revelation about going abroad?

"Vicki, what's going on?" asked Sian.

"Nothing. I need to get out of here for a bit; stay out of Tommy's way until they send him to jail. Before that, he might decide to do something to get back at me for grassing on him."

"Oh, right. I suppose. What about me, Vicki? Am I going to be safe? I helped you too," said Sian, her anxiety and discomfort growing.

"You'll be fine, Sian. Tommy doesn't know you had anything to do with any of this. You don't need to worry about him. You really don't. I promise."

"Where are you going?"

"Spain. You remember Carla from the dance classes?"

"Aye, sort of."

"Anyway, she's half-Spanish and she moved back to Madrid last year. She's been on at me to go out and visit, so I've arranged to stay with her for a bit. Get some sun, chill out. It's just what I need. All this upset with Tommy and Cath has been so stressful."

Sian looked into her friend's face. Vicki looked as beautiful as she always did but there was something missing in her eyes. The spark and mischief had gone. She couldn't be too surprised about that, though. What Vicki had gone through - finding out about her mum and dad and everything else - was awful. Anybody, no matter how tough they liked to make out they were, would have been affected by it.

"If you'd said, I could have come with you," said Sian.

Vicki hugged her tight. Sian felt the warm glow she always did when they touched. She would have given anything to be able to kiss Vicki; to tell her how she felt. But she didn't.

"Oh, Sian. You're such a sweetheart. I'll give you the address. If you can get time off work, I can meet you out there. Ok?"

That seemed fair enough to Sian.

"Ok, I'll take you to the airport. Are you ready now, then?"

"Give me two minutes. I just need to go powder my nose and then we'll be off."

24.

I've woken up in a hospital bed. There's bleeping machinery with various bits of tubing and wires connecting me to it. I can hear voices but nothing distinct; nobody is actually talking to me. I can't move much. My head feels as heavy as a bowling ball and my tongue is stuck to the roof of my mouth. I've definitely felt better.

I can see movement in the corridor. I seem to be in a small room, which is odd as I don't belong to any private health care scheme. I don't really know what's happened. My brain is still under the influence of legal narcotics. I begin to recall things.

A dark room, gun shots, pain.

Vicki.

Betrayal.

I hear the door open.

"Oh my god, Ross, you're awake!"

It's my mum. She runs to me, but the wires and tubes and who knows what else prevent her from making any greater physical contact than to grab my hand and squeeze.

She kisses the back of my hand and starts to cry.

"Oh, Ross, thank god you're ok. I thought I might have ..." she says, before her voice is choked out by a sob.

A nurse comes into the room. She checks readings, takes my pulse, sticks a thermometer in my ear and begins to scribble notes.

"Hi, Ross. How are you feeling, my lovely?" she asks.

I can't speak but I make a dry rasping sound which is meant to be: "Like dung, how do you think I feel?"

"Do you want some water, honey?"

No shit Sherlock, I think, as I nod.

The cold liquid feels amazing as it slides down my

gullet. It's not the elixir of life, though. It's just water. I'm not ready to throw back the covers and walk out of there.

"Ross, what happened? I was so scared," says my mum.

"Mrs Fleming, I think you need to let Ross rest. He's got a long fight ahead of him and he'll need all the energy he can get, ok?" says Dorothy, the nurse assigned to look after me.

"Yes, of course. I'm sorry. Ok, Ross, I'm going to go and get a wee bite to eat. I'm starving. I'll see you in a little while, darling. You get some sleep and we can talk later."

She kisses me on the forehead and lightly shifts my fringe. I glance out of the open door behind her. There's a cop sitting outside. I don't know why. I feel dog-tired as I notice Dorothy boost my meds. *There's no place like home* I think, as I drift off.

It's dark when I wake again. The only company I have is the collection of machines on stilts, helping to mend and monitor my broken body. I feel afraid, vulnerable. I don't really know why.

There's a glow from behind the curtains of my room, the night shift going about their duties. I remember the cop and wonder if he's still stationed outside. I notice the call button alongside me on the bed. I press it, hoping someone will bring more water.

The nurse doesn't take long to respond. It's a different one than before. This one's younger, called Michelle, and - although much prettier than Dorothy - she's not as considerate. Doesn't say much, does the necessary checks on my vital signs, lets me sip some water and then buggers off.

The medication boost is more subtle this time. I drift again, into the welcoming arms of Morpheus.

The light hurts the back of my eyes. I'm squinting, mouth drier than a Bedouin's sandal. I reach for the drink on the table next to my bed, wince and groan. My mum helps me, directs the straw to my mouth.

"There you go, son. You have a wee drink," she says, in the voice I recognise from when I was a sickly wee bairn.

"How are you, Ross?"

"I'm ok. I think," I manage to croak.

"That's good, son. I was so worried about you. What happened? Can you remember anything about what happened?"

"Not really, Ma. What have the doctors said?"

"You were incredibly lucky," she says, stifling a huge sob, taking a deep breath. "Another inch to the left and you might have been paralysed. The bullet went right through you, damaged your kidney a bit but the doc says that should be ok. Anyway, you've got two of them, you could afford to lose one if you had to. You've also got a broken rib. Otherwise, you're fine."

She sits back and dabs her nose and eyes with a paper tissue.

My mind is still a bit foggy and I'm trying to piece together various snippets of memory into usable chunks, to form a storyline.

There's a room with a hard floor, a gun, white boiler suits; Tommy Stevens.

Vicki.

Betrayal.

My next visitors are DI Pinky and DS Perky. I think the police must have gone to 'Dicks R Us' for this pair. Buy one bell-end; get another one free.

My history of interaction with the constabulary is riddled with misunderstanding and ill-will on both sides. They come in looking to nail me for Tommy's killing. In the hours since I came back to conscious thought, I've been bracing myself for what to tell the cops. I know Vicki has shafted me; used me as a pawn to get to Tommy and exact her revenge. The easy option is to try and drag her into this but I can't bring myself to grass her up.

"Look, I've told you, I don't know what happened. All

I remember is being shot by Tommy, I've got no idea who killed him."

DI Pinky is actually called DI Clarke, he's English. The sidekick is called Ferris; he's Scottish and looks a bit of a smug bastard. It's Clarke who does all the talking and he's a steely son-of-a-bitch.

"Really, son. We find you lying on the floor, holding the gun used to kill Tommy Stevens and you're claiming someone else shot him?"

"Aye, that's what I said."

"So, how is it you came to get gunpowder residue on your hands?"

I feel genuinely puzzled by this and just shrug. That hurts like a bastard. I keep forgetting that moving suddenly, no matter how minimal the motion, is like driving a stake through my torso.

"What is it, son? Surprised by that? Didn't think we'd have remembered to do the test? Well, sorry to disappoint you but we did and you're the only guy in the frame as things stand. Forensics have been over the room and the only prints are from you and Tommy. The only bullets come from your gun and his. I'll tell you what I think happened, shall I?" he says, a sly smile spreading over his face. Ferris looks on, impassive, taking notes.

"I'm going to go out on a fucking limb here and assume you're going to tell me, whether I'm interested in your horseshit theory or not," I reply, reciprocating in the sly smile stakes.

"Ah, got a smart mouth. Well, that won't stop you getting ten years for manslaughter, son. You see, I reckon you shot Stevens in self-defence. I don't know what the dispute was about but, knowing that scumbag, it'll be something to do with drugs, money or women. Maybe a combination of all three. So, unless you want to put a name to this mystery killer, I think you should get ready for a long stretch in the Bar-L."

He pauses for dramatic effect, looks at Ferris, then

back to me.

"Of course, there's also the bullet we found in your pocket, wrapped in tissue paper. We haven't matched it to a body yet but we will, son. I can guarantee you I won't rest until I find out who took that slug before you retrieved it."

If I was feeling blasé before, I'm not now. I have a vague recollection of Tommy saying he'd taken care of Ralph's body and kept the cops out of it but I can't be one hundred per cent sure. My memories have been scrambled by the trauma and the drugs.

"I don't know anything about a bullet," I say but I'm not sure I'd believe me if I was the cop.

He's preparing the next onslaught of scepticism when Dorothy, being the caring, sharing type of nurse that she is, decides it's time for my visitors to leave. I couldn't agree more.

"Detective Inspector, I think that's enough for now. Ross is still very weak from losing all that blood and the operation. If you need to speak to him again, please come back tomorrow."

The cops stand and excuse themselves, promising they will indeed be back the next day. I'm so happy. But, I don't spend too long thinking about that pair of knob-ends coming back.

Only one thing fills my thoughts.

Vicki.

Betrayal.

25.

Vicki liked the two-tone blue seats, supported by banana-yellow poles, in the carriages on the Madrid underground. They made it look a bit like a long, snaking climbing-frame from a children's playground. It was a great service too: affordable, efficient, clean and comfortable. Glasgow's equivalent service paled in comparison. Madrid's Metro made the 'Clockwork Orange', as Glaswegians liked to call it, seem less like something you'd find in a playground and more like something from a child's bedroom.

The city of Madrid really appealed to Vicki. The cobalt sky framed impressive architecture: colonial mansion houses, towering Gothic cathedrals and ornate street furniture, regularly punctuated by green spaces and parks. Walking about in summer dresses, feeling her Vitamin D deficiency reducing, wearing shades and browsing designer boutiques, she could sense the worrying ambivalence of her feelings after the shooting fading away.

She was standing outside a very fancy designer store, admiring her bronzed reflection in the window, when the phone rang.

"Hi, Sian!"

"Vicki, what the fuck is going on? I just found out Tommy's dead and Ross is in hospital."

Sian sounded borderline hysterical and Vicki felt cornered, ill-prepared to respond without making things worse or having her story straight. Her first instinct was to bluff it.

"What? Oh my, God! That's fucking terrible! I had no idea, Sian," she said, trying to make herself sound as shocked as possible. It seemed to throw Sian off at first, as there was complete silence from her friend for a few seconds.

"Are you fucking kidding me, Vicki? You're actually going to try and tell me you knew nothing about this; had nothing to do with it even?"

This time, Sian's voice was edged with disgust and anger.

"What do you mean, Sian?" said Vicki, digging ever deeper.

"Oh, Christ. I thought we were friends but you're lying through your fucking teeth to me. I helped you with this. I picked you up from that warehouse. I knew you were up to something when you wanted to go to the airport straight afterwards. What the hell happened? If the police come calling, what am I supposed to tell them? I could go to jail, Vicki. We both could."

It looked like all the money Tommy spent on acting lessons for Vicki in her teens may not have been a great investment after all. How should she deal with this? Sian was right in a way. She had helped Vicki, but now it sounded like she might become a loose cannon; a liability, likely to drop them both in the shit.

"Sian, listen to me. Calm down. This is stupid. I didn't kill Tommy or shoot Ross. Why would I do something so insane?"

There was another silence. Vicki could sense Sian computing her response, but was thrown by what she said.

"How did you know Ross was shot?"

"Eh?"

"How did you know Ross was shot? I never said that. I didn't know that. I just heard he was in hospital. Oh, fuck ..."

"Sian, please, this is silly, Tommy liked to carry a gun, I just assumed it would be that," said Vicki, scrambling to rescue the situation.

"No, this isn't right. You were supposed to call the police so they would stop Tommy from hurting Ross. Why didn't you stay there if Tommy had a gun? Why did you leave Ross with him? And, how did Tommy die? If he had a gun and Ross got shot, who shot Tommy?"

"I, I ..."

"No, no, no. Oh, fuck! Oh, shit!"

Vicki felt like her head might explode.

"I can't talk about this right now, Sian. You have to believe me, I didn't have anything to do with this. I don't understand why you'd think I did. You're supposed to be my friend. I'm sorry, I have to go."

Vicki cancelled the call, felt her legs go weak and staggered. A passing stranger caught her by the elbow and put his arm round her middle before she could fall.

"Hey, you ok, *señora?*" he asked, in a heavy accent.

Vicki shrugged him off.

"Yes, I'm fine. *Gracias.*"

She gathered herself and began to walk. She needed to think, to decide what to do.

Sian looked at the blank screen of the phone in her hand, incredulous, terrified.

Her stomach started to behave like it was auditioning for some kind of circus act. She rushed for the toilet, gripping the edge of the bowl, retching. After a series of dry heaves, the churning nausea subsided. She sat on the tiled floor of the bathroom, back against the side of the bath, head filling with dark scenarios. Tears dragged make-up down her face.

Maybe Vicki was right. Sian must be a bad friend for thinking her capable of something so awful, but she knew when she was being played. The tone of voice, the slip of the tongue, the sudden termination of their call, throwing the guilt back at Sian: all consistent with having something to hide. It was obvious now: there was only one way to get to the truth.

Sian called the hospital and asked about visiting times.

26.

I've had another visit from the two little pigs, been through the same rigmarole as before. They asked me stuff, I gave them shitty answers, they got frustrated. We parted on bad terms. I can sense they're going to be causing me a lot more trouble before long but they can wait. I've got trouble of another kind to deal with right now - my Ma.

The honeymoon's over for her, as far as doling out sympathy and being thankful I'm alive is concerned. She's moved onto indignation and outrage at my continued involvement with Tommy Stevens. She's upset that I lied to her. She's upset that I didn't listen to her about how dangerous he was. There's a lot of 'I-told-you-so' going on. This particular lecture has been going on for about fifteen minutes. I've decided not to confront her yet about Paul Stevens' claims regarding my dad. I don't have the energy to argue, make a coherent case or get angry. The showdown can wait, because Sian McDonald just walked into the room.

My mum stops her tirade, looking puzzled but pleased at the same time. It's fair to say Sian is a striking looking girl. I think my Ma has put two and two together and come up with buying a hat and becoming a grandma.

"Hello?" she says.

"Hi, I'm Sian, I'm a friend of Ross's. Is it ok if I come and say hello?" says Sian.

She's trying to smile but there's a haunted look about her; something dark around her eyes; a hollow sound to her voice. She's usually a bubbly kind of a character.

"Yes, of course dear. Come in. I'm Anne, I'm Ross's mum," she says.

"Thanks,"

Sian sits in a seat beside the bed.

"How are you, Ross?" she asks. Her voice cracks. It looks like she might start to cry.

"Aye, I'm getting there, Sian. Thanks."

"I'm sorry," she says, this time her voice barely more than a wisp in the air.

My mum senses the moment is right for her to give us some space. Her motive is likely misguided, but it's welcome nonetheless.

"Can I get you a wee cup of tea, Sian?"

"Eh, that would be nice. Just milk, thanks, Mrs Fleming."

"Ok, and please call me Anne, by the way."

Sian gives her a slight smile and my Ma gets up and heads out of the room.

"Hey, Sian, what are you doing here?" I ask her.

"Ross, I'm so sorry, I had no idea what she was really planning."

The confusion on my face must be obvious and she bows her head, avoiding eye-contact.

"She told me it would all be fine, that you'd be fine and Tommy would end up in the jail. I never thought for one minute she would ... you know ..."

I can't formulate a response for a few seconds. I'm letting this sink in. Vicki must have suckered Sian into helping her too. Like me, she never saw the boot coming towards her face.

Betrayal.

"Where is she?" I eventually ask.

"Spain. Madrid."

"Spain? What the fuck is she doing there?"

"Aye, well, I thought she was going on a wee holiday to get her head together while the police dealt with Tommy. She's staying with a lassie we used to dance with who lives there. Although, I think maybe she's actually gone on the run," she says, a tear escaping the corner of her eye as she looks away again.

I let what she's telling me run through my head a few times. The past couple of days I've been trying to decide what to do - waiting for Vicki to redeem herself, show some contrition, prove she still means something to me. It's never going to happen. I can see that. She's manipulated me for the last time. I know what I need to do.

"Sian, listen, I need to talk to her but she won't answer her phone."

This is a lie. I haven't tried phoning her yet but I'm pretty sure she wouldn't answer me if I did call, so I need another way in.

"Have you got an address maybe, or an alternative number in Spain?"

She looks at me askance, "What are you going to do, Ross?"

"Nothing stupid. Don't worry, I only want to speak to her, that's all. Maybe, when I've recovered, I'll go out there and see her. I want to look her in the eye and ask her why she did it. I want a fucking apology for putting me through all this shit. She nearly killed me, for fuck's sake!"

Betrayal.

I let my voice rise, hoping anger might convince her to comply.

"Ok," she says. She takes a piece of paper out of her bag and proceeds to scribble something down. She hands it to me and stands up as my Ma comes back into the room.

"I'm sorry, Anne, thanks for getting the tea but I need to go," says Sian and heads for the door. She stops, turns back to give me a small wave and another of those smiles, "See you around, Ross. Take care of yourself."

"Thanks, Sian. I'll be fine. You take care too."

She goes out and my mum has a look on her face like someone pissed on her chips.

"So, who was that, Ross?"

"That's Gerry McDonald's sister. You remember Big Mac don't you?"

"Oh, aye, the lad you used to go clubbing with sometimes?"

"That's him. She heard I was poorly and thought she would come and see if I was ok."

She didn't seem too convinced, but didn't push it.

Sian's interruption used up most of the visiting time and before my Ma could launch into any more criticism of my recent lifestyle choices, Dorothy was shooing her away. I was falling in love with that women. An angel indeed.

The lights are out. The glow behind the curtain remains. I feel the turmoil and conflict finally still in my head.

I'll make the call.

It's the only way to deal with this. I don't need the police or the full force of the law to help me deal with this problem.

I'll make the call.

One call.

That's all it will take and we'll be square.

I take my phone out from under my pillow, rub my thumb across the screen.

One call.

I punch in the number.

The phone rings.

"Hello?"

"You know I didn't shoot him, don't you? Vicki did it. She set me up."

Silence.

"I know where she is."

"Where?"

"Spain."

"You got the details?"

"Aye, but Paul, nothing sadistic, ok? Quick and easy."

"Don't worry about that, son. That's not your concern."

"And that's us square?"
"That's us square."
I hang up.
Betrayal.
It's a two-way street.

27.

Life is back to normal. Unfortunately for me that means no job, no money, crushing boredom and my Ma on my back, getting on at me about having no money and no job. I'm back doing the dance with the Social regarding the efforts I make to find work. For a while, my injuries meant I didn't have to try too hard to find a job but the most recent medical assessment deemed me 'fit to undertake any available work'. It's a shame, but I don't think I can add my stint working for Tommy Stevens to my CV. At least, I don't reckon it will be any help in offsetting the damage my criminal record and lack of qualifications do as far as prospective employers are concerned. A reference wouldn't be too easy to come by either. I'm doing what I need to do to maintain the meagre benefits on offer: doing the training courses, attending the reviews, filling out the application forms. Both parties know it's futile but there are boxes to be ticked and politicians to answer to.

I think about Vicki every day and regret what I did almost as much as I'm glad about it. There's no denying she deserved it; no question she betrayed me in the worst possible way and likely would have done so again. Probably without stopping to think first. The thing is, I can't help worrying about how Paul Stevens went about it, how unpleasant he made her last moments. Dark, troubling dreams have begun to plague my nights.

I can see she played me from the start but, even though I know this, I can't stop thinking about that flurry of sexual passion in her flat. It fills my every waking hour. Endless bouts of *what if*, *maybe*, and *if only* turn in my head like a relentless merry-go-round that I can't stop or get down from. I know it's pointless to torture myself like this.

Knowing it's pointless doesn't prevent it from happening.

I haven't heard from Paul Stevens and I've avoided contacting Sian. So far. At least twice a day I'm tempted to track Sian down but, up until now, I've resisted. I don't want her to know anything about what I did and I really don't want gloating confirmation of Vicki's fate from that spiteful cripple. But, just like the *what ifs*, it rotates constantly on that fairground ride inside my head.

I think I might be going mad.

I don't go out much. There are some compulsory trips to the Social to keep them happy, and voluntary trips to the Post Office to withdraw my paltry benefit money. I'm totally broke but my reclusive behaviour is not all about the lack of money - it runs deeper than that. I sense I'm being judged, sneered at, considered inferior to others. It feels like people know what I did and they don't approve. But even this crash in my self-esteem and ego is only a small part of the problem. Not going out is nearly all about fear. I find myself gripped with paranoia about Paul Stevens deciding we're not square after all. It's hard to trust him. He's not what anyone would consider a stand-up guy, a model citizen. I'm pretty sure all that honour amongst thieves and word-is-my-bond bullshit is just that – bullshit. I look over my shoulder almost as much as I watch where I'm going. I see danger in every stranger's eyes.

It feels like I might be going mad.

The cops are still waiting in the wings. So far, they've not found enough evidence to proceed with anything. My brief seems to think they'll give the manslaughter thing a miss. Nobody in authority grieves for Tommy Stevens - just one more scumbag out of the way. It looks like a straightforward self-defence case and I'd most likely walk. They could make better use of the money it would cost them to find out. I get the impression DI Clarke would give up a night of passion with Angelina Jolie if he could get me for Ralph's murder, but it seems as if Tommy did a good job of the disposal. He's still only got a bullet wrapped in tissue paper and no victim to match it to.

Every day I brace myself for that knock on the door when he turns up and, with a huge grin on his face, tells me he's found Bonner's body.

There's a good chance I'm going mad.

It's Saturday, about six o'clock. My Ma has dragged me to the shops. She's noticed how down I'm getting and thought she could cheer me up with some retail therapy. I'm trying to act grateful but it was never my preferred method for elevating my mood. Amongst so many people, the paranoia is shredding me.

I've still not had the energy or the desire to face her up about my dad. I'm a bottler of emotions by nature. It goes into the pot, gets stirred along with all the other shit.

"I'm going to buy a couple of birthday cards in here," she says. "Why don't you go and get yourself a coffee?"

She hands me a fiver and I manage a weak smile of gratitude.

I wander along the concourse, feel the weight of the other shoppers' judgement crush down on me, see shadows shift in the background. I manage to negotiate the queue and get a cappuccino. I don't even really want a coffee but, what the hell, it will pass a few minutes and stop my Ma from fussing over me.

As ever, once I'm still, my mind begins to turn my problems around, over and over. I stare into the coffee cup at the chocolate pattern in the froth. I tune out from the sounds around me, focus on the froth, let my eyes trace the outline of the feather or fern or whatever the pattern is meant to be. I need the turmoil to stop for just a few minutes. I need peace.

"Hello, Ross."

Startled, I don't know whether I'm consumed more by terror or by disbelief, relief or desire. It feels like it might be all four in unison.

"Hi," is all I can muster.

She's as beautiful as ever. Her once-golden hair is dark, matching her eyes.

"How are you?" she asks.

I can't answer. I manage a shrug and a small shake of my head. A tear slides down my cheek but I didn't sense it getting ready to fall. She reaches across the table and puts her hand on mine. I feel the world sweeping away from me.

"It's ok, Ross. I just came to tell you that I know it was you who told Paul - but I forgive you. Let's be honest, I kind of asked for it."

I look into her eyes and the tears are flowing freely now. I can't control them. She squeezes my hand, smiles.

"Don't cry, Ross, please. People are looking. They'll think I'm dumping you or something."

She laughs.

I can't join in.

"I'm sorry how things turned out," she whispers.

I look down into the froth, tracing the chocolate pattern with my eyes.

The tears stop.

I look up and she's gone.

My Ma sits down in front of me and puts her coffee on the table.

"You ok, son?" she asks, frowning.

I smile and nod but I can't tell her the truth.

I think I must be going mad.

Thank You!

Thank you for buying this book - I really hope you enjoyed it. If you did, it would be great if you could leave a review on Amazon.

You can visit my website at *petercarroll.ravencrestbooks.com*, and while you are there, I'd be delighted if you also subscribed to my blog. That way, I can keep you up to date with future books and other writing adventures.

Look out for my other novels *Stark Contrasts, Stark Choices, In Many Ways* and *Pandora's Pitbull* which are all available from Amazon.

All the best

Peter

THE FIRST IN THE ADAM STARK DETECTIVE SERIES

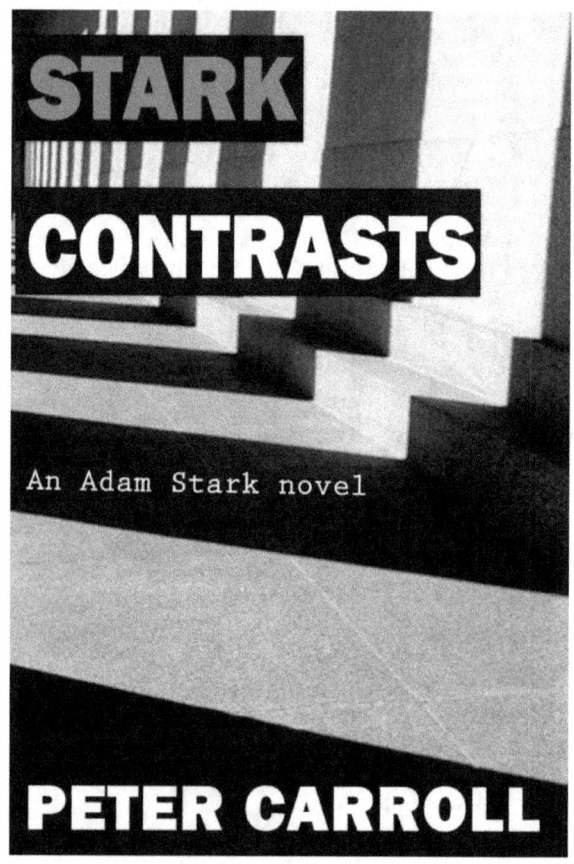

It drives you mad right? All those anti-social behaviours you endure every day in a big city - inconsideration, selfishness, low level violence, intimidation. You wish you had the nerve, the strength of character to intervene, to speak out, to do ... something. Well, someone in London has had enough and they are doing something about it.

Something drastic.

As punishments escalate in severity and the press make a champion of this anti-hero, Detective Inspector Adam Stark is desperately trying to make sense of what's going on. Random, unconnected victims, excessive retribution, red herrings, kidnap, mutilation, mistaken identity, gangsters, revenge and murder. Things are getting totally out of hand.

Stark needs to nail this sociopath with a social conscience, but the case might just be running away from him - heading toward a brutal and bloody conclusion.

Thriller of the Month - May 2013 at e-thriller.com

"Entertaining reading and will make you think twice again before tailgating on the roads, spitting gum or playing your music too loud on public transport!"

Rating: Great satisfaction for any reader!

If you have a smart phone, scan the barcode for a link to "Stark Contrasts"

THE SECOND IN THE ADAM STARK DETECTIVE SERIES

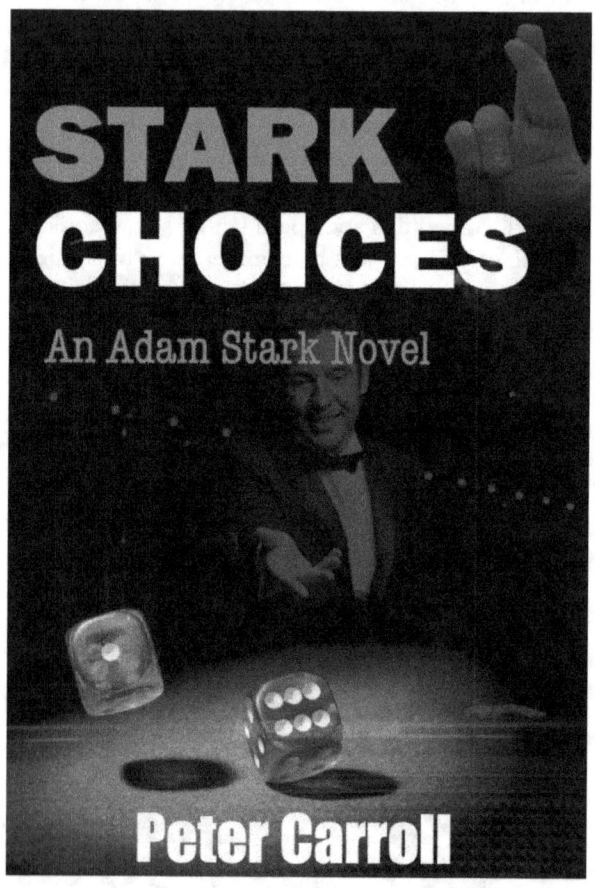

DI Adam Stark has left London and his overbearing boss, returned to his home town of Alloa, hoping things might be quieter and to spend a bit of time with his Ma.

Meanwhile, Stella McDuff has just won millions on the lottery. It's the only good luck she's had in her entire life.

She has plans to escape to London, leaving her life of drudgery, her thoughtless children and brutish husband, Billy, behind. Stark knows the McDuffs well. Billy and his brother Malky are arch-enemies from childhood and they're not pleased to see him again.

Stella is rich, she can almost taste her freedom, but winning that amount of money has awakened a few green-eyed monsters. It's not long before she's facing every parent's worst nightmare and Stark is dealing with missing persons, kidnap, ransom and murder. So much for the quiet life back home.

Be careful what you wish for..

If you have a smart phone, scan the barcode for a link to "Stark Choices"

In Many Ways

A young man is abducted and mutilated for talking out of turn, and a policeman is murdered as a result – all in a day's work for Danny O'Neill, Scotland's most notorious gangster.

Meanwhile, small-time drug dealer and shop worker Davie Argyle has just crossed O'Neill's path. Davie has been waiting a long time for this. He needs to swallow his pride and convince O'Neill to trust him. Thing is, can he stay alive long enough for his plan to work?

Torture, murder, rock n roll and bloody revenge ensue as pasts unfurl and long-held secrets reveal themselves. In many ways, it was only a matter of time until it all kicked off...

Thriller Of The Month on www.e-thriller.com *"... following firmly in the footsteps of the pioneers of 'Tartan Noir' trail blazed by Ian Rankin and his erstwhile detective John Rebus, Peter Carroll takes us away from the prim and proper streets of the capital Edinburgh and takes us instead to the mean streets of Glasgow. Recommended and riveting reading from a relatively new author."*

If you have a smart phone, scan the barcode for a link to "In Many Ways"

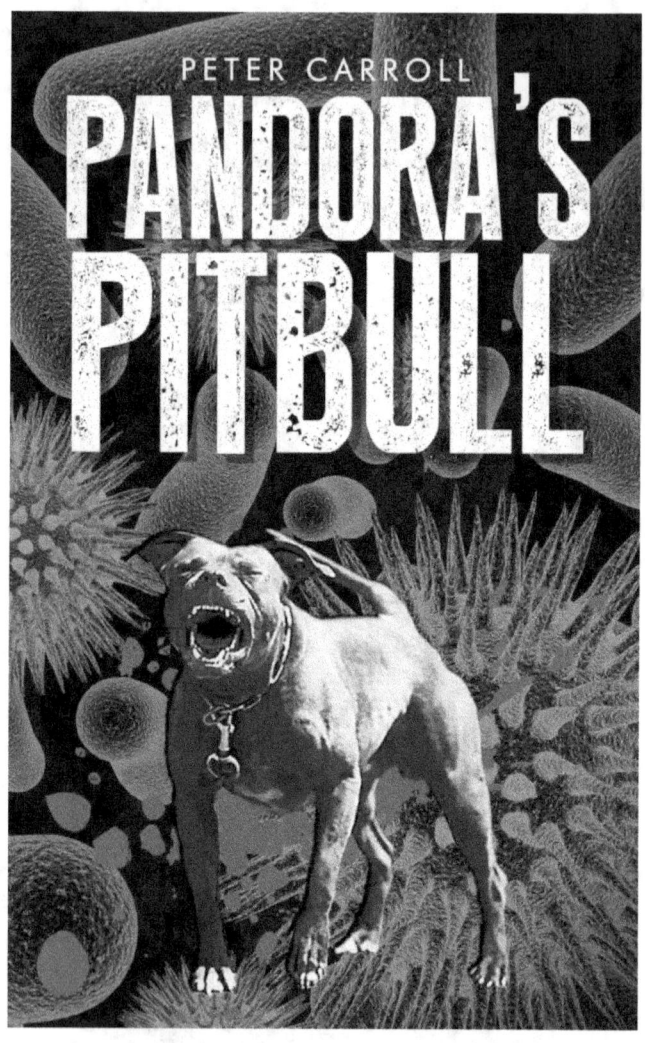

PETER CARROLL

PANDORA'S PITBULL

Two clandestine world's have collided - with disastrous
consequences.

A fighting dog, kidnapped and used in a top secret
experiment, is free and carrying a virus. A virus like

nothing that's gone before. A virus that's spreading through Scotland unchecked.

As society implodes and people refuse to die a normal death, the fates of a small boy, a young woman, a soldier and the very country they live in will hang in the balance.

A new evil has been unleashed on the world but it might be too late to put the lid back on this particular box ...
Indie Book of the Month August 2012

"Fantastic book! I absolutely love Carroll's writing style. Carroll is a true talent at writing intelligent and witty material."
RA Stephenson author of "Collapse (New America #1)"

If you have a smart phone, scan the barcode for a link to "Pandora's Pitbull"

About The Author

Peter Carroll is a Scotsman with a penchant for black humour and gritty realism. As well as writing, he's passionate about nature conservation and music.

Peter has four novels under his belt so far: crime thriller "In Many Ways", apocalyptic horror "Pandora's Pitbull", and the Adam Stark detective series, "Stark Contrasts " and "Stark Choices "

"Stark Choices" is his fourth novel.

Contact Details

Visit the authors website:
petercarroll.ravencrestbooks.com

www.twitter.com/petercarroll10

Cover designed by: Raven Crest Books

Published by: Raven Crest Books
www.ravencrestbooks.com

Follow us on Twitter:
www.twitter.com/lyons_dave